TALES FROM THE "WHITE HART"

BOOKS BY ARTHUR C. CLARKE

NONFICTION

Interplanetary Flight
The Exploration of Space
The Exploration of the Moon
Going into Space
The Coast of Coral
The Making of a Moon
The Reefs of Taprobane
Voice Across the Sea
The Challenge of the Spaceship
The Challenge of the Sea
Profiles of the Future
Voices from the Sky
The Promise of Space
Report on Planet Three
The First Five Fathoms
Boy Beneath the Sea
Indian Ocean Adventure
Indian Ocean Treasure
The Treasure of the Great Reef
The View from Serendip
1984: Spring—A Choice of Futures

With the Editors of "Life"
Man and Space

With the Astronauts
First on the Moon

With Robert Silverberg
Into Space

With Chelsey Bonestell
Beyond Jupiter

With Simon Welfare & John Fairley
Arthur C. Clarke's Mysterious World

With Peter Hyams
The Odyssey File

FICTION

Islands in the Sky
Prelude to Space
Against the Fall of Night
The Sands of Mars
Childhood's End
Expedition to Earth
Earthlight
Reach for Tomorrow
The City and the Stars
Tales from the "White Hart"
The Deep Range
The Other Side of the Sky
*Across the Sea of Stars
A Fall of Moondust
*From the Ocean, From the Stars
Tales of Ten Worlds
Dolphin Island
Glide Path
The Lion of Comarre
*The Nine Billion Names of God
*Prelude to Mars
The Lost Worlds of 2001
The Wind from the Sun
Rendezvous with Rama
Imperial Earth
The Fountains of Paradise
2010: Odyssey Two
The Songs of Distant Earth
2061: Odyssey Three
3001: The Final Odyssey

With Stanley Kubrick
2001: A Space Odyssey

With Gentry Lee
Cradle
Rama II

*Anthologies

TALES FROM THE "WHITE HART"

Arthur C. Clarke

BALLANTINE BOOKS • NEW YORK

A Del Rey® Book
Published by The Ballantine Publishing Group

 Published in the United States by The Ballantine Publishing Group, a division of Random House, Inc., New York, and simultaneously in Canada by Random House of Canada Limited, Toronto.

http://www.randomhouse.com

Library of Congress Catalog Card Number: 98-96308

ISBN: 0-345-43072-7

Cover design by Min Choi
Background cover photo © Mehau Kulyk, Science Source/Photo Researchers
Text design by Jie Yang

Manufactured in the United States of America

First Mass Market Edition: January 1957
First Ballantine Books Trade Edition: October 1998
10 9 8 7 6 5 4 3 2 1

To Lew
and his Thursday night customers

Contents

Preface

These stories were written in spurts and spasms between 1953 and 1956 at such diverse spots on the globe as New York, Miami, Colombo, London, Sydney, and various other locations whose names now escape me. In some cases the geographical influence is obvious, though curiously enough I had never visited Australia when "What Goes Up. . . ." was written

It seems to me that there is room—one might even say a long unfelt want—for what might be called the "tall" science-fiction story. By this I mean stories that are *intentionally* unbelievable; not, as is too often the case, unintentionally so. At the same time, I should hate to say exactly where the Great Divide of plausibility comes in these tales, which range from the perfectly possible to the totally improbable.

In at least two cases, science has practically caught up with me in the few years since I wrote these stories. The technique described in "Big Game Hunt" has already been used on monkeys, so there is no reason to suppose that it could not be adapted to other creatures. For a more successful conclusion to this particular hunt—and the rest of the quotation from Herman Melville—I refer you to my novel "The Deep Range."

It is in the field touched upon in "Patent Pending," however, that the most hair-raising discovery has been made—a discovery which should stop anyone worrying about such minor menaces as the hydrogen bomb. The first report of the work that may end our civilization will be found in James Old's article "Pleasure Centers in the Brain" (*Scientific American*, October 1956). Briefly, it has been found that an electric current flowing into a certain area in the brain of a rat can produce intense pleasure. So much so, in fact, that when the rat learns that it can stimulate itself at will by pushing a little pedal, it loses interest in anything else—even in food. I quote: "Hungry rats ran faster to reach an electric stimulator than they did to reach food. Indeed, a hungry animal often ignored available food in favor of the pleasure of stimulating itself electrically. Some rats . . . stimulated their brains more than 2,000 times per hour for 24 consecutive hours!"

The article concludes with these ominous words: "Enough of the brain-stimulating work has been repeated on monkeys . . . to indicate that our general conclusions can very likely be generalized eventually to human beings—with modifications, of course."

Of course.

For the record (written, not electroencephalographic) I believe the first writers to use the theme of "Patent Pending" were Fletcher Pratt and Laurence Manning, back in the '30's. And quite recently, in "The Big Ball of Wax," Shepherd Mead had given it a much more ribald treatment than mine. I thought his book very funny before I read Mr. Old's article. You may still do so.

Another item for which I cannot claim originality is the newspaper quotation in "Cold War." It is perfectly genuine. It may even have been true.

I must confess that, having chosen the title of this volume some years ago, I was a little disconcerted when Sprague de

Camp and Fletcher Pratt brought out their "Tales from Gavagan's Bar." But as most of the odd goings-on at Mr. Cohan's establishment are concerned with the supernatural, I feel that there is plenty of room for both taverns—especially as they are separated by the width of the Atlantic.

Finally, a word to any readers of my (pause for modest cough) more serious works, who may be distressed to find me taking the universe so light-heartedly after my earlier preoccupation with such themes as the Destiny of Man and the Exploration of Space (Advt.) My only excuse is that for some years I've been irritated by critics who keep claiming that science fiction and humor are incompatible.

Now they have a chance to prove it and shut up.

New York,
October 1956

TALES FROM THE "WHITE HART"

Silence Please

You come upon the "White Hart" quite unexpectedly in one of these anonymous little lanes leading down from Fleet Street to the Embankment. It's no use *telling* you where it is: very few people who have set out in a determined effort to get there have actually arrived. For the first dozen visits a guide is essential: after that you'll probably be all right if you close your eyes and rely on instinct. Also—to be perfectly frank—we don't want any more customers, at least on *our* night. The place is already uncomfortably crowded. All that I'll say about its location is that it shakes occasionally with the vibration of newspaper presses, and that if you crane out of the window of the gent's room you can just see the Thames.

From the outside, it looks like any other pub—as indeed it is for five days of the week. The public and saloon bars are on the ground floor: there are the usual vistas of brown oak panelling and frosted glass, the bottles behind the bar, the handles of the beer engines . . . nothing out of the ordinary at all. Indeed, the only concession to the twentieth century is the juke box in the public bar. It was installed during the war in a laughable attempt to make G.I.'s feel at home, and one of the first things we did was to make sure there was no danger of its ever working again.

At this point I had better explain who "we" are. That is not as easy as I thought it was going to be when I started, for a complete catalogue of the "White Hart's" clients would probably be impossible and would certainly be excruciatingly tedious. So all I'll say at this point is that "we" fall into three main classes. First there are the journalists, writers and editors. The journalists, of course, gravitated here from Fleet Street. Those who couldn't make the grade fled elsewhere: the tougher ones remained. As for the writers, most of them heard about us from other writers, came here for copy, and got trapped.

Where there are writers, of course, there are sooner or later editors. If Drew, our landlord, got a percentage on the literary business done in his bar, he'd be a rich man. (We suspect he is a rich man, anyway.) One of our wits once remarked that it was a common sight to see half a dozen indignant authors arguing with a hard-faced editor in one corner of the "White Hart," while in another, half a dozen indignant editors argued with a hard-faced author.

So much for the literary side: you will have, I'd better warn you, ample opportunities for close-ups later. Now let us glance briefly at the scientists. How did *they* get in here?

Well, Birkbeck College is only across the road, and King's is just a few hundred yards along the Strand. That's doubtless part of the explanation, and again personal recommendation had a lot to do with it. Also, many of our scientists are writers, and not a few of our writers are scientists. Confusing, but we like it that way.

The third portion of our little microcosm consists of what may be loosely termed "interested laymen." They were attracted to the "White Hart" by the general brouhaha, and enjoyed the conversation and company so much that they now come along regularly every Wednesday—which is the day when we all get together. Sometimes they can't stand the pace and fall by the wayside, but there's always a fresh supply.

With such potent ingredients, it is hardly surprising that Wednesday at the "White Hart" is seldom dull. Not only have some remarkable stories been told there, but remarkable things have *happened* there. For example, there was the time when Professor ———, passing through on his way to Harwell, left behind a brief-case containing—well, we'd better not go into that, even though we did so at the time. And most interesting it was, too. . . . Any Russian agents will find me in the corner under the dartboard. I come high, but easy terms can be arranged.

Now that I've finally thought of the idea, it seems astonishing to me that none of my colleagues has ever got round to writing up these stories. Is it a question of being so close to the wood that they can't see the trees? Or is it lack of incentive? No, the last explanation can hardly hold: several of them are quite as hard up as I am, and have complained with equal bitterness about Drew's "NO CREDIT" rule. My only fear, as I type these words on my old Remington Noiseless, is that John Christopher or George Whitley or John Beynon are already hard at work using up the best material. Such as, for instance, the story of the Fenton Silencer. . . .

I don't know when it began: one Wednesday is much like another and it's hard to tag dates on to them. Besides, people may spend a couple of months lost in the "White Hart" crowd before you first notice their existence. That had probably happened to Harry Purvis, because when I first came aware of him he already knew the names of most of the people in our crowd. Which is more than I do these days, now that I come to think of it.

But though I don't know *when*, I know exactly *how* it all started. Bert Huggins was the catalyst, or, to be more accurate, his voice was. Bert's voice would catalyse anything. When he indulges in a confidential whisper, it sounds like a sergeant major drilling an entire regiment. And when he lets himself go, conversation languishes elsewhere while we all wait for those cute little bones in the inner ear to resume their accustomed places.

He had just lost his temper with John Christopher (we all do this at some time or other) and the resulting detonation had disturbed the chess game in progress at the back of the saloon bar. As usual, the two players were surrounded by backseat drivers, and we all looked up with a start as Bert's blast whammed overhead. When the echoes died away, someone said: "I wish there was a way of shutting him up."

It was then that Harry Purvis replied: "There is, you know."

Not recognising the voice, I looked round. I saw a small, neatly-dressed man in the late thirties. He was smoking one of those carved German pipes that always makes me think of cuckoo clocks and the Black Forest. That was the only unconventional thing about him: otherwise he might have been a minor Treasury official all dressed up to go to a meeting of the Public Accounts Committee.

"I beg your pardon?" I said.

He took no notice, but made some delicate adjustments to his pipe. It was then that I noticed that it wasn't, as I'd thought at first glance, an elaborate piece of wood carving. It was something much more sophisticated—a contraption of metal and plastic like a small chemical engineering plant. There were even a couple of minute valves. My God, it *was* a chemical engineering plant. . . .

I don't goggle any more easily than the next man, but I made no attempt to hide my curiosity. He gave me a superior smile.

"All for the cause of science. It's an idea of the Biophysics Lab. They want to find out exactly what there is in tobacco smoke—hence these filters. You know the old argument—*does* smoking cause cancer of the tongue, and if so, how? The trouble is that it takes an awful lot of—er—distillate to identify some of the obscurer bye-products. So we have to do a lot of smoking."

"Doesn't it spoil the pleasure to have all this plumbing in the way?"

"I don't know. You see, I'm just a volunteer. I don't smoke."

"Oh," I said. For the moment, that seemed the only reply. Then I remembered how the conversation had started.

"You were saying," I continued with some feeling, for there was still a slight tintinus in my left ear, "that there was some way of shutting up Bert. We'd all like to hear it—if that isn't mixing metaphors somewhat."

"I was thinking," he replied, after a couple of experimental sucks and blows, "of the ill-fated Fenton Silencer. A sad story—yet, I feel, one with an interesting lesson for us all. And one day—who knows?—someone *may* perfect it and earn the blessings of the world."

Suck, bubble, bubble, *plop*. . . .

"Well, let's hear the story. When did it happen?"

He sighed.

"I'm almost sorry I mentioned it. Still, since you insist—and, of course, on the understanding that it doesn't go beyond these walls."

"Er—of course."

"Well, Rupert Fenton was one of our lab assistants. A very bright youngster, with a good mechanical background, but, naturally, not very well up in theory. He was always making gadgets in his spare time. Usually the idea was good, but as he was shaky on fundamentals the things hardly ever worked. That didn't seem to discourage him: I think he fancied himself as a latter-day Edison, and imagined he could make his fortune from the radio tubes and other oddments lying around the lab.

As his tinkering didn't interfere with his work, no-one objected: indeed, the physics demonstrators did their best to encourage him, because, after all, there is something refreshing about any form of enthusiasm. But no-one expected he'd ever get very far, because I don't suppose he could even integrate *e* to the *x*."

"Is such ignorance *possible*?" gasped someone.

"Maybe I exaggerate. Let's say *x e* to the *x*. Anyway, all his knowledge was entirely practical—rule of thumb, you know. Give him a wiring diagram, however complicated, and he could make the apparatus for you. But unless it was something *really* simple, like a television set, he wouldn't understand how it worked. The trouble was, he didn't realise his limitations. And that, as you'll see, was most unfortunate.

"I think he must have got the idea while watching the Honours Physics students doing some experiments in acoustics. I take it, of course, that you all understand the phenomenon of interference?"

"Naturally," I replied.

"Hey!" said one of the chess-players, who had given up trying to concentrate on the game (probably because he was losing.) "*I* don't."

Purvis looked at him as though seeing something that had no right to be around in a world that had invented penicillin.

"In that case," he said coldly, "I suppose I had better do some explaining." He waved aside our indignant protests. "No, I insist. It's precisely those who don't understand these things who need to be told about them. If someone had only explained the theory to poor Fenton while there was still time. . . ."

He looked down at the now thoroughly abashed chess-player.

"I do not know," he began, "if you have ever considered the nature of *sound*. Suffice to say that it consists of a series of waves moving through the air. Not, however, waves like those on the surface of the sea—oh dear no! *Those* waves are up and down movements. Sound waves consist of alternate compressions and rarefactions."

"Rare-what?"

"Rarefactions."

"Don't you mean 'rarefications'?"

"I do not. I doubt if such a word exists, and if it does, it shouldn't," retorted Purvis, with the *aplomb* of Sir Alan Herbert dropping a particularly revolting neologism into his killing-bottle. "Where was I? Explaining sound, of course. When we make any sort of noise, from the faintest whisper to that concussion that went past just now, a series of pressure changes moves through the air. Have you ever watched shunting engines at work on a siding? You see a perfect example of the same kind of thing. There's a long line of goods-wagons, all coupled together. One end gets a bang, the first two trucks move together—and then you can see the compression wave moving right along the line. Behind it the reverse thing happens—the rarefaction—I repeat, *rarefaction*—as the trucks separate again.

"Things are simple enough when there is only one source of sound—only one set of waves. But suppose you have two wave-patterns, moving in the same direction? That's when interference arises, and there are lots of pretty experiments in elementary physics to demonstrate it. All we need worry about here is the fact—which I think you will all agree is perfectly obvious—that if one could get two sets of waves *exactly* out of step, the total result would be precisely zero. The compression pulse of one sound wave would be on top of the rarefaction of another—net result—no change and hence no sound. To go back to my analogy of the line of wagons, it's as if you gave the last truck a jerk and a push simultaneously. Nothing at all would happen.

"Doubtless some of you will already see what I am driving at, and will appreciate the basic principle of the Fenton Silencer. Young Fenton, I imagine, argued in this manner. 'This world of ours,' he said to himself, 'is too full of noise. There would be a fortune for anyone who could invent a really perfect silencer. Now, what would that imply . . . ?'

"It didn't take him long to work out the answer: I told you he was a bright lad. There was really very little in his pilot model. It consisted of a microphone, a special amplifier, and a pair of loudspeakers. Any sound that happened to be about was picked up by the mike, amplified and *inverted* so that it was exactly out of phase with the original noise. Then it was pumped out of the speakers, the original wave and the new one cancelled out, and the net result was silence.

"Of course, there was rather more to it than that. There had to be an arrangement to make sure that the cancelling wave was just the right intensity—otherwise you might be worse off than when you started. But these are technical details that I won't bore you with. As many of you will recognise, it's a simple application of negative feed-back."

"Just a moment!" interrupted Eric Maine. Eric, I should mention, is an electronics expert and edits some television paper or other. He's also written a radio play about space-flight, but that's another story. "Just a moment! There's something wrong here. You *couldn't* get silence that way. It would be impossible to arrange the phase . . ."

Purvis jammed the pipe back in his mouth. For a moment there was an ominous bubbling and I thought of the first act of "Macbeth." Then he fixed Eric with a glare.

"Are you suggesting," he said frigidly, "that this story is untrue?"

"Ah—well, I won't go as far as that, but . . ." Eric's voice trailed away as if he had been silenced himself. He pulled an old envelope out of his pocket, together with an assortment of resistors and condensers that seemed to have got entangled in his handkerchief, and began to do some figuring. That was the last we heard from him for some time.

"As I was saying," continued Purvis calmly, "*that's* the way Fenton's Silencer worked. His first model wasn't very powerful, and it couldn't deal with very high or very low notes. The result was rather odd. When it was switched on, and someone tried to talk, you'd hear the two ends of the spectrum—a faint bat's squeak, and a kind of low rumble. But he soon got over that by using a more linear circuit (dammit, I can't help using *some* technicalities!) and in the later model he was able to produce complete silence over quite a large area. Not merely an ordinary room, but a full-sized hall. Yes. . . .

"Now Fenton was not one of these secretive inventors who won't tell anyone what they are trying to do, in case their ideas are stolen. He was all too willing to talk. He discussed his ideas with the staff and with the students, whenever he could get anyone to listen. It so happened that one of the first people to whom he demonstrated his improved Silencer was a young Arts student called—I think—Kendall, who was taking Physics as a subsidiary subject. Kendall was much impressed by the Silencer, as well he might be. But he was not thinking, as you may have imagined, about its commercial possibilities, or the boon it would bring to the outraged ears of suffering humanity. Oh dear no! He had quite other ideas.

"Please permit me a slight digression. At College we have a flourishing Musical Society, which in recent years has grown in numbers to such an extent that it can now tackle the less monumental symphonies. In the year of which I speak, it was embarking on a very ambitious enterprise. It was going to produce a new opera, a work by a talented young composer whose name it would not be fair to mention, since it is now well-known to you all. Let us call him Edward England. I've forgotten the title of the work, but it was one of these stark dramas of tragic love which, for some reason I've never been able to understand, are supposed to be less ridiculous with a musical accompaniment than without. No doubt a good deal depends on the music.

"I can still remember reading the synopsis while waiting for the curtain to go up, and to this day have never been able to decide whether the libretto was meant seriously or not. Let's see—the period was the late Victorian era, and the main characters were Sarah Stampe, the passionate postmistress, Walter Partridge, the saturnine gamekeeper, and the squire's son, whose name I forget. It's the old story of the eternal triangle, complicated by the villager's resentment of change—in this case, the new telegraph system, which the local crones predict will Do Things to the cows' milk and cause trouble at lambing time.

"Ignoring the frills, it's the usual drama of operatic jealousy. The squire's son doesn't want to marry into the Post Office, and the gamekeeper, maddened by his rejection, plots revenge. The tragedy rises to its dreadful climax when poor Sarah, strangled with parcel tape, is found hidden in a mailbag in the Dead Letter Department. The villagers hang Partridge from the nearest telegraph pole, much to the annoyance of the linesmen. He was supposed to sing an aria while he was being hung: *that* is one thing I regret missing. The squire's son takes to drink, or the Colonies, or both: and that's that.

"I'm sure you're wondering where all this is leading: please bear with me for a moment longer. The fact is that while this synthetic jealousy was being rehearsed, the real thing was going on back-stage. Fenton's friend Kendall had been spurned by the young lady who was to play Sarah Stampe. I don't think he was a particularly vindictive person, but he saw an opportunity for a unique revenge. Let us be frank and admit that college life *does* breed a certain irresponsibility—and in identical circumstances, how many of *us* would have rejected the same chance?

"I see the dawning comprehension on your faces. But we, the audience, had no suspicion when the overture started on that memorable day. It was a most distinguished gathering: everyone was there, from the Chancellor downwards. Deans and professors were two a penny: I never did discover how so many people had been bullied into coming. Now that I come to think of it, I can't remember what I was doing there myself.

"The overture died away amid cheers, and, I must admit, occasional cat-calls from the more boisterous members of the audience. Perhaps I do them an injustice: they may have been the more musical ones.

"Then the curtain went up. The scene was the village square at Doddering Sloughleigh, *circa* 1860. Enter the heroine, reading the postcards in the morning's mail. She comes across a letter addressed to the young squire and promptly bursts into song.

"Sarah's opening aria wasn't quite as bad as the overture, but it was grim enough. Luckily, we were to hear only the first few bars. . . .

"Precisely. We need not worry about such details as how Kendall had talked the ingenuous Fenton into it—if, indeed, the inventor realised the use to which his device was being applied. All I need say is that it was a most convincing demonstration. There was a sudden, deadening blanket of silence, and Sarah Stampe just faded out like a TV programme when the sound is turned off. Everyone was frozen in their seats, while the singer's lips went on moving silently. Then she too realised what had happened. Her mouth opened in what would have been a piercing scream in any other circumstances, and she fled into the wings amid a shower of postcards.

"Thereafter, the chaos was unbelievable. For a few minutes

everyone must have thought they had lost the sense of hearing, but soon they were able to tell from the behaviour of their companions that they were not alone in their deprivation. Someone in the Physics Department must have realised the truth fairly promptly, for soon little slips of paper were circulating among the V.I.P.'s in the front row. The Vice-Chancellor was rash enough to try and restore order by sign-language, waving frantically to the audience from the stage. By this time I was too sick with laughter to appreciate such fine details.

"There was nothing for it but to get out of the hall, which we all did as quickly as we could. I think Kendall had fled—he was so overcome by the effect of the gadget that he didn't stop to switch it off. He was afraid of staying around in case he was caught and lynched. As for Fenton—alas, we shall never know *his* side of the story. We can only reconstruct the subsequent events from the evidence that was left.

"As I picture it, he must have waited until the hall was empty, and then crept in to disconnect his apparatus. We heard the explosion all over the college."

"The *explosion*?" someone gasped.

"Of course. I shudder to think what a narrow escape we all had. Another dozen decibels, a few more phons—and it might have happened while the theatre was still packed. Regard it, if you like, as an example of the inscrutable workings of providence that only the inventor was caught in the explosion. Perhaps it was as well: at least he perished in the moment of achievement, and before the Dean could get at him."

"Stop moralising, man. What happened?"

"Well, I told you that Fenton was very weak on theory. If he'd gone into the mathematics of the Silencer he'd have found his mistake. The trouble is, you see, that one can't *destroy* energy. Not even when you cancel out one train of waves by another. All that happens then is that the energy you've neutralized accumulates *somewhere else*. It's rather like sweeping up all the dirt in a room—at the cost of an unsightly pile under the carpet.

"When you look into the theory of the thing, you'll find that Fenton's gadget wasn't a silencer so much as a *collector* of sound. All the time it was switched on, it was really absorbing sound energy. And at that concert, it was certainly going flat out. You'll understand what I mean if you've ever looked at one of Edward England's scores. On top of that, of course, there was all the noise the audience was making—or I should say was *trying* to make—during the resultant panic. The total amount of energy must have been terrific, and the poor Silencer had to keep on sucking it up. Where did it go? Well, I don't know the circuit details—probably into the condensers of the power pack. By the time Fenton started to tinker with it again, it was like a loaded bomb. The sound of his approaching footsteps was the last straw, and the overloaded apparatus could stand no more. It blew up."

For a moment no-one said a word, perhaps as a token of respect for the late Mr. Fenton. Then Eric Maine, who for the last ten minutes had been muttering in the corner over his calculations, pushed his way through the ring of listeners. He held a sheet of paper thrust aggressively in front of him.

"Hey!" he said. "I was right all the time. The thing couldn't work. The phase and amplitude relations. . . ."

Purvis waved him away.

"That's just what I've explained," he said patiently. "You should have been listening. Too bad that Fenton found out the hard way."

He glanced at his watch. For some reason, he now seemed in a hurry to leave.

"My goodness! Time's getting on. One of these days, remind

me to tell you about the extraordinary thing we saw through the new proton microscope. That's an even more remarkable story."

He was half way through the door before anyone else could challenge him. Then George Whitley recovered his breath.

"Look here," he said in a perplexed voice. "How is it that we never heard about this business?"

Purvis paused on the threshold, his pipe now burbling briskly as it got into its stride once more. He glanced back over his shoulder.

"There was only one thing to do," he replied. "We didn't want a scandal—*de mortuis nil nisi bonum*, you know. Besides, in the circumstances, don't you think it was highly appropriate to—ah—*hush* the whole business up? And a very good night to you all."

Big Game Hunt

Although by general consent Harry Purvis stands unrivalled among the "White Hart" *clientele* as a purveyor of remarkable stories (some of which, we suspect, may be slightly exaggerated) it must not be thought that his position has never been challenged. There have even been occasions when he has gone into temporary eclipse. Since it is always entertaining to watch the discomfiture of an expert, I must confess that I take a certain glee in recalling how Professor Hinckelberg disposed of Harry on his own home ground.

Many visiting Americans pass through the "White Hart" in the course of the year. Like the residents, they are usually scientists or literary men, and some distinguished names have been recorded in the visitors' book that Drew keeps behind the bar. Sometimes the newcomers arrive under their own power, diffidently introducing themselves as soon as they have the opportunity. (There was the time when a shy Nobel Prize winner sat unrecognised in a corner for an hour before he plucked up enough courage to say who he was.) Others arrive with letters of introduction, and not a few are escorted in by regular customers and then thrown to the wolves.

Professor Hinckelberg glided up one night in a vast fish-tailed Cadillac he'd borrowed from the fleet in Grosvenor Square. Heaven only knows how he had managed to insinuate it through the side streets that lead to the "White Hart," but amazingly enough all the fenders seemed intact. He was a large lean man, with that Henry-Ford-Wilbur-Wright kind of face that usually goes with the slow, taciturn speech of the sun-tanned pioneer. It didn't in Professor Hinckelberg's case. He could talk like an L.P. record on a 78 turntable. In about ten seconds we'd discovered that he was a zoologist on leave of absence from a North Virginia college, that he was attached to the Office of Naval Research on some project to do with plankton, that he was tickled pink with London and even liked English beer, that he'd heard about us through a letter in *Science* but couldn't believe we were true, that Stevenson was O.K. but if the Democrats wanted to get back they'd better import Winston, that he'd like to know what the heck was wrong with all our telephone call boxes and could he retrieve the small fortune in coppers of which they had mulcted him, that there seemed to be a lot of empty glasses around and how about filling them up, boys?

On the whole the Professor's shock-tactics were well received, but when he made a momentary pause for breath I thought to myself "Harry'd better look out. This guy can talk rings around him." I glanced at Purvis, who was only a few feet away from me, and saw that his lips were pursed into a slight frown. I sat back luxuriously and awaited results.

As it was a fairly busy evening, it was quite sometime before Professor Hinckelberg had been introduced to everybody. Harry, usually so forward at meeting celebrities, seemed to be keeping out of the way. But eventually he was cornered by Arthur Vincent, who acts as informal club secretary and makes sure that everyone signs the visitors' book.

"I'm sure you and Harry will have a lot to talk about," said

Arthur, in a burst of innocent enthusiasm. "You're both scientists, aren't you? And Harry's had some most extraordinary things happen to him. Tell the Professor about the time you found that U 235 in your letterbox. . . ."

"I don't think," said Harry, a trifle too hastily, "that Professor—ah—Hinckelberg wants to listen to my little adventure. I'm sure he must have a lot to tell *us*."

I've puzzled my head about that reply a good deal since then. It wasn't in character. Usually, with an opening like this, Purvis was up and away. Perhaps he was sizing up the enemy, waiting for the Professor to make the first mistake, and then swooping in to the kill. If that was the explanation, he'd misjudged his man. He never had a chance, for Professor Hinckelberg made a jet-assisted take-off and was immediately in full flight.

"Odd you should mention that," he said. "I've just been dealing with a most remarkable case. It's one of these things that can't be written up as a proper scientific paper, and this seems a good time to get it off my chest. I can't often do that, because of this darned security—but so far no-one's gotten round to classifying Dr. Grinnell's experiments, so I'll talk about them while I can."

Grinnell, it seemed, was one of the many scientists trying to interpret the behaviour of the nervous system in terms of electrical circuits. He had started, as Grey Walter, Shannon and others had done, by making models that could reproduce the simpler actions of living creatures. His greatest success in this direction had been a mechanical cat that could chase mice and could land on its feet when dropped from a height. Very quickly, however, he had branched off in another direction owing to his discovery of what he called "neural induction." This was, to simplify it greatly, nothing less than a method of actually *controlling* the behaviour of animals.

It had been known for many years that all the processes that take place in the mind are accompanied by the production of minute electric currents, and for a long time it has been possible to record these complex fluctuations—though their exact interpretation is still unknown. Grinnell had not attempted the intricate task of analysis; what he had done was a good deal simpler, though its achievement was still complicated enough. He had attached his recording device to various animals, and thus been able to build up a small library, if one could call it that, of electrical impulses associated with their behaviour. One pattern of voltage might correspond to a movement to the right, another with travelling in a circle, another with complete stillness, and so on. That was an interesting enough achievement, but Grinnell had not stopped there. By "playing back" the impulses he had recorded, he could compel his subjects to repeat their previous actions—whether they wanted to or not.

That such a thing might be possible in theory almost any neurologist would admit, but few would have believed that it could be done in practice owing to the enormous complexity of the nervous system. And it was true that Grinnell's first experiments were carried out on very low forms of life, with relatively simple responses.

"I saw only one of his experiments," said Hinckelberg. "There was a large slug crawling on a horizontal piece of glass, and half a dozen tiny wires led from it to a control panel which Grinnell was operating. There were two dials—that was all—and by suitable adjustments he could make the slug move in any direction. To a layman, it would have seemed a trivial experiment, but I realised that it might have tremendous implications. I remember telling Grinnell that I hoped his device could never be applied to human beings. I'd been reading Orwell's "1984" and I could just imagine what Big Brother would do with a gadget like this.

"Then, being a busy man, I forgot all about the matter for a year. By the end of that time, it seems, Grinnell had improved his apparatus considerably and had worked up to more complicated organisms, though for technical reasons he had restricted himself to invertebrates. He had now built up a substantial store of 'orders' which he could then play back to his subjects. You might think it surprising that such diverse creatures as worms, snails, insects, crustaceans and so on would be able to respond to the same electrical commands, but apparently that was the case.

"If it had not been for Dr. Jackson, Grinnell would probably have stayed working away in the lab for the rest of his life, moving steadily up the animal kingdom. Jackson was a very remarkable man—I'm sure you must have seen some of his films. In many circles he was regarded as a publicity-hunter rather than a real scientist, and academic circles were suspicious of him because he had far too many interests. He'd led expeditions into the Gobi Desert, up the Amazon, and had even made one raid on the Antarctic. From each of these trips he had returned with a best-selling book and a few miles of Kodachrome. And despite reports to the contrary, I believe he *had* obtained some valuable scientific results, even if they were slightly incidental.

"I don't know how Jackson got to hear of Grinnell's work, or how he talked the other man into co-operating. He could be very persuasive, and probably dangled vast appropriations before Grinnell's eyes—for he was the sort of man who could get the ear of the trustees. Whatever happened, from that moment Grinnell became mysteriously secretive. All we knew was that he was building a much larger version of his apparatus, incorporating all the latest refinements. When challenged, he would squirm nervously and say, 'We're going big game hunting.'

"The preparations took another year, and I expect that Jackson—who was always a hustler—must have been mighty impatient by the end of that time. But at last everything was ready. Grinnell and all his mysterious boxes vanished in the general direction of Africa.

"*That* was Jackson's work. I suppose he didn't want any premature publicity, which was understandable enough when you consider the somewhat fantastic nature of the expedition. According to the hints with which he had—as we later discovered—carefully mislead us all, he hoped to get some really remarkable pictures of animals in their wild state, using Grinnell's apparatus. I found this rather hard to swallow, unless Grinnell had somehow succeeded in linking his device to a radio transmitter. It didn't seem likely that he'd be able to attach his wires and electrodes to a charging elephant. . . .

"They'd thought of that, of course, and the answer seems obvious now. Sea water is a good conductor. They weren't going to Africa at all, but were heading out into the Atlantic. But they hadn't lied to us. They were after big game, all right. The biggest game there is. . . .

"We'd never have known what happened if their radio operator hadn't been chattering to an amateur friend over in the States. From his commentary it's possible to guess the sequence of events. Jackson's ship—it was only a small yacht, bought up cheaply and converted for the expedition—was lying-to not far from the Equator off the west coast of Africa, and over the deepest part of the Atlantic. Grinnell was angling: his electrodes had been lowered into the abyss, while Jackson waited impatiently with his camera.

"They waited a week before they had a catch. By that time, tempers must have been rather frayed. Then, one afternoon on a perfectly calm day, Grinnell's meters started to jump. Something was caught in the sphere of influence of the electrodes.

"Slowly, they drew up the cable. Until now, the rest of the

crew must have thought them mad, but everyone must have shared their excitement as the catch rose up through all those thousands of feet of darkness until it broke surface. Who can blame the radio operator if, despite Jackson's orders, he felt an urgent need to talk things over with a friend back on the safety of dry land?

"I won't attempt to describe what they saw, because a master has done it before me. Soon after the report came in, I turned up my copy of 'Moby Dick' and re-read the passage; I can still quote it from memory and don't suppose I'll ever forget it. This is how it goes, more or less:

" 'A vast pulpy mass, furlongs in length, of a glancing cream-colour, lay floating on the water, innumerable long arms radiating from its centre, curling and twisting like a nest of anacondas, as if blindly to catch at any hapless object within reach.'

"Yes: Grinnell and Jackson had been after the largest and most mysterious of all living creatures—the giant squid. Largest? Almost certainly: *Bathyteuthis* may grow up to a hundred feet long. He's not as heavy as the sperm whales who dine upon him, but he's a match for them in length.

"So here they were, with this monstrous beast that no human being had ever before seen under such ideal conditions. It seems that Grinnell was calmly putting it through its paces while Jackson ecstatically shot off yards of film. There was no danger, though it was twice the size of their boat. To Grinnell, it was just another mollusc that he could control like a puppet by means of his knobs and dials. When he had finished, he would let it return to its normal depths and it could swim away again, though it would probably have a bit of a hangover.

"What one wouldn't give to get hold of that film! Altogether apart from its scientific interest, it would be worth a fortune in Hollywood. You must admit that Jackson knew what he was doing: he'd seen the limitations of Grinnell's apparatus and put it to its most effective use. What happened next was not his fault."

Professor Hinckelberg sighed and took a deep draught of beer, as if to gather strength for the finale of his tale.

"No, if anyone is to blame it's Grinnell. Or, I should say, it *was* Grinnell, poor chap. Perhaps he was so excited that he overlooked a precaution he would undoubtedly have taken in the lab. How otherwise can you account for the fact that he didn't have a spare fuse handy when the one in the power supply blew out?

"And you can't really blame *Bathyteuthis*, either. Wouldn't *you* have been a little annoyed to be pushed about like this? And when the orders suddenly ceased and you were your own master again, you'd take steps to see it remained that way. I sometimes wonder, though, if Jackson stayed filming to the very end. . . ."

Patent Pending

There are no subjects that have not been discussed, at some time or other, in the saloon bar of the "White Hart"—and whether or not there are ladies present makes no difference whatsoever. After all, they came in at their own risk. Three of them, now I come to think of it, have eventually gone out again with husbands. So perhaps the risk isn't on their side at all. . . .

I mention this because I would not like you to think that all our conversations are highly erudite and scientific, and our activities purely cerebral. Though chess is rampant, darts and shove-ha'penny also flourish. The *Times Literary Supplement*, the *Saturday Review*, the *New Statesman* and the *Atlantic Monthly* may be brought in by some of the customers, but the same people are quite likely to leave with the latest issue of *Staggering Stories of Pseudoscience*

A great deal of business also goes on in the obscurer corners of the pub. Copies of antique books and magazines frequently change hands at astronomical prices, and on almost any Wednesday at least three well-known dealers may be seen smoking large cigars as they lean over the bar, swapping stories with Drew. From time to time a vast guffaw announces the *dénouement* of some anecdote and provokes a flood of anxious enquiries from patrons who are afraid they may have missed something. But, alas, delicacy forbids that I should repeat any of these interesting tales here. Unlike most things in this island, they are not for export. . . .

Luckily, no such restrictions apply to the tales of Mr. Harry Purvis, B.Sc. (at least), Ph.D. (probably) F.R.S. (personally I don't think so, though it *has* been rumoured). None of them would bring a blush to the cheeks of the most delicately nurtured maiden aunts, should any still survive in these days.

I must apologise. This is too sweeping a statement. There was one story which might, in some circles, be regarded as a little daring. Yet I do not hesitate to repeat it, for I know that you, dear reader, will be sufficiently broadminded to take no offence.

It started in this fashion. A celebrated Fleet Street reviewer had been pinned into a corner by a persuasive publisher, who was about to bring out a book of which he had high hopes. It was one of the riper productions of the deep and decadent South—a prime example of the "and-then-the-house-gave-another-lurch-as-the-termites-finished-the-east-wing" school of fiction. Eire had already banned it, but that is an honour which few books escape nowadays, and certainly could not be considered a distinction. However, if a leading British newspaper could be induced to make a stern call for its suppression, it would become a best-seller overnight. . . .

Such was the logic of its publisher, and he was using all his wiles to induce co-operation. I heard him remark, apparently to allay any scruples his reviewer friend might have, "Of course not! If they can understand it, they *can't* be corrupted any further!" And then Harry Purvis, who has an uncanny knack of following half a dozen conversations simultaneously, so that he can insert himself in the right one at the right time, said in his peculiarly penetrating and non-interruptable voice: "Censorship does raise some very difficult problems doesn't it? I've always argued that there's an inverse correlation between a country's degree of civilisation and the restraints it puts on its press."

A New England voice from the back of the room cut in: "On *that* argument, Paris is a more civilised place then Boston."

"Precisely," answered Purvis. For once, he waited for a reply.

"O.K." said the New England voice mildly. "I'm not arguing. I just wanted to check."

"To continue," said Purvis, wasting no more time in doing so, "I'm reminded of a matter which has not yet concerned the censor, but which will certainly do so before long. It began in France, and so far has remained there. When it *does* come out into the open, it may have a greater impact on our civilisation than the atom bomb.

"Like the atom bomb, it arose out of equally academic research. *Never,* gentlemen, underestimate science. I doubt if there is a single field of study so theoretical, so remote from what is laughingly called everyday life, that it may not one day produce something that will shake the world.

"You will appreciate that the story I am telling you is, for once in a while, second-hand. I got it from a colleague at the Sorbonne last year while I was over there at a scientific conference. So the names are all fictitious: I was told them at the time, but I can't remember them now.

"Professor—ah—Julian was an experimental physiologist at one of the smaller, but less impecunious, French universities. Some of you may remember that rather unlikely tale we heard here the other week from that fellow Hinckelberg, about his colleague who'd learned how to control the behaviour of animals through feeding the correct currents into their nervous systems. Well, if there *was* any truth in that story—and frankly

I doubt it—the whole project was probably inspired by Julian's papers in *Comptes Rendus*.

"Professor Julian, however, never published his most remarkable results. When you stumble on something which is really terrific, you don't rush into print. You wait until you have overwhelming evidence—unless you're afraid that someone else is hot on the track. Then you may issue an ambiguous report that will establish your priority at a later date, without giving too much away at the moment—like the famous cryptogram that Huygens put out when he detected the rings of Saturn.

"You may well wonder what Julian's discovery was, so I won't keep you in suspense. It was simply the natural extension of what man has been doing for the last hundred years. First the camera gave us the power to capture scenes. Then Edison invented the phonograph, and sound was mastered. Today, in the talking film, we have a kind of mechanical memory which would be inconceivable to our forefathers. But surely the matter cannot rest there. Eventually science must be able to catch and store thoughts and sensations themselves, and feed them back into the mind so that, whenever it wishes, it can repeat any experience in life, down to its minutest detail."

"That's an old idea!" snorted someone. "See the 'feelies' in 'Brave New World.'"

"All good ideas have been thought of by somebody before they are realised," said Purvis severely. "The point is that what Huxley and others had talked about, Julian actually did. My goodness, there's a pun there! Aldous—Julian—oh, let it pass!

"It was done electronically, of course. You all know how the encephalograph can record the minute electrical impulses in the living brain—the so-called 'brain waves,' as the popular press calls them. Julian's device was a much subtler elaboration of this well-known instrument. And, having recorded cerebral impulses, he could play them back again. It sounds simple, doesn't it? So was the phonograph, but it took the genius of Edison to think of it.

"And now, enter the villain. Well, perhaps that's too strong a word, for Professor Julian's assistant Georges—Georges Dupin—is really quite a sympathetic character. It was just that, being a Frenchman of a more practical turn of mind than the Professor, he saw at once that there were some milliards of francs involved in this laboratory toy.

"The first thing was to get it out of the laboratory. The French have an undoubted flair for elegant engineering, and after some weeks of work—with the full co-operation of the Professor—Georges had managed to pack the "play-back" side of the apparatus into a cabinet no larger than a television set, and containing not very many more parts.

"Then Georges was ready to make his first experiment. It would involve considerable expense, but as someone so rightly remarked you cannot make omelettes without breaking eggs. And the analogy is, if I may say so, an exceedingly apt one.

"For Georges went to see the most famous *gourmet* in France, and made an interesting proposition. It was one that the great man could not refuse, because it was so unique a tribute to his eminence. Georges explained patiently that he had invented a device for registering (he said nothing about storing) sensations. In the cause of science, and for the honour of the French *cuisine*, could he be privileged to analyse the emotions, the subtle nuances of gustatory discrimination, that took place in Monsieur le Baron's mind when he employed his unsurpassed talents? Monsieur could name the restaurant, the *chef* and the menu—everything would be arranged for his convenience. Of course, if he was too busy, no doubt that well-known epicure, Le Compte de—

"The Baron, who was in some respects a surprisingly coarse man, uttered a word not to be found in most French dictionaries. '*That* cretin!' he exploded. 'He would be happy on English cooking! No, *I* shall do it.' And forthwith he sat down to compose the menu, while Georges anxiously estimated the cost of the items and wondered if his bank balance would stand the strain. . . .

"It would be interesting to know what the chef and the waiters thought about the whole business. There was the Baron, seated at his favourite table and doing full justice to his favourite dishes, not in the least inconvenienced by the tangle of wires that trailed from his head to that diabolical-looking machine in the corner. The restaurant was empty of all other occupants, for the last thing Georges wanted was premature publicity. This had added very considerably to the already distressing cost of the experiment. He could only hope that the results would be worth it.

"They were. The only way of *proving* that, of course, would be to play back Georges' 'recording.' We have to take his word for it, since the utter inadequacy of words in such matters is all too well-known. The Baron *was* a genuine connoisseur, not one of those who merely pretend to powers of discrimination they do not possess. You know Thurber's 'Only a naive domestic Burgundy, but I think you'll admire its presumption.' The Baron would have known at the first sniff whether it was domestic or not—and if it had been presumptious he'd have smacked it down.

"I gather that Georges had his money's worth out of that recording, even though he had not intended it merely for personal use. It opened up new worlds to him, and clarified the ideas that had been forming in his ingenious brain. There was no doubt about it: all the exquisite sensations that had passed through the Baron's mind during the consumption of that Lucullan repast had been captured, so that anyone else, however untrained they might be in such matters, could savour them to the full. For, you see, the recording dealt purely with emotions: intelligence did not come into the picture at all. The Baron needed a lifetime of knowledge and training before he could *experience* these sensations. But once they were down on tape, anyone, even if in real life they had no sense of taste at all, could take over from there.

"Think of the glowing vistas that opened up before Georges' eyes! There were other meals, other gourmets. There were the collected impressions of all the vintages of Europe—what would connoisseurs not pay for them? When the last bottle of a rare wine had been broached, its incorporeal essence could be preserved, as the voice of Melba can travel down the centuries. For, after all, it was not the wine itself that mattered, but the sensations it evoked. . . .

"So mused Georges. But this, he knew, was only a beginning. The French claim to logic I have often disputed, but in Georges' case it cannot be denied. He thought the matter over for a few days: then he went to see his *petite dame*.

" 'Yvonne, *ma cheri*,' he said, 'I have a somewhat unusual request to make of you. . . .' "

Harry Purvis knew when to break off in a story. He turned to the bar and called, "Another Scotch, Drew." No-one said a word while it was provided.

"To continue," said Purvis at length, "the experiment, unusual though it was, even in France, was successfully carried out. As both discretion and custom demanded, all was arranged in the lonely hours of the night. You will have gathered already that Georges was a persuasive person, though I doubt if Mam'selle needed much persuading.

"Stifling her curiosity with a sincere but hasty kiss, Georges saw Yvonne out of the lab and rushed back to his apparatus. Breathlessly, he ran through the playback. It worked—not that he had ever had any real doubts. Moreover—do please remember I have only my informant's word for this—it was indistinguishable from the real thing. At that moment something approaching religious awe overcame Georges. This was, without a doubt, the greatest invention in history. He would be immortal as well as wealthy, for he had achieved something of which all men had dreamed, and had robbed old age of one of its terrors. . . .

"He also realised that he could now dispense with Yvonne, if he so wished. This raised implications that would require further thought. *Much* further thought.

"You will, of course, appreciate that I am giving you a highly condensed account of events. While all this was going on, Georges was still working as a loyal employee of the Professor, who suspected nothing. As yet, indeed, Georges had done little more than any research worker might have in similar circumstances. His performances had been somewhat beyond the call of duty, but could all be explained away if need be.

"The next step would involve some very delicate negotiations and the expenditure of further hard-won francs. Georges now had all the material he needed to prove, beyond a shadow of doubt, that he was handling a very valuable commercial property. There were shrewd businessmen in Paris who would jump at the opportunity. Yet a certain delicacy, for which we must give him full credit, restrained Georges from using his second—er—recording as a sample of the wares his machine could purvey. There was no way of disguising the personalities involved, and Georges was a modest man. 'Besides,' he argued, again with great good sense, 'when the gramophone company wished to make a *disque*, it does not enregister the performance of some amateur musician. *That* is a matter for professionals. And so, *ma foi*, is *this*.' Whereupon, after a further call at his bank, he set forth again for Paris.

"He did not go anywhere near the Place Pigalle, because that was full of Americans and prices were accordingly exorbitant. Instead, a few discreet enquiries and some understanding cab-drivers took him to an almost oppressively respectable suburb, where he presently found himself in a pleasant waiting room, by no means as exotic as might have been supposed.

"And there, somewhat embarrassed, Georges explained his mission to a formidable lady whose age one could have no more guessed than her profession. Used though she was to unorthodox requests, *this* was something she had never encountered in all her considerable experience. But the customer was always right, as long as he had the cash, and so in due course everything was arranged. One of the young ladies and her boy friend, an *apache* of somewhat overwhelming masculinity, travelled back with Georges to the provinces. At first they were, naturally, somewhat suspicious, but as Georges had already found, no expert can ever resist flattery. Soon they were all on excellent terms. Hercule and Susette promised Georges that they would give him every cause for satisfaction.

"No doubt some of you would be glad to have further details, but you can scarcely expect me to supply them. All I can say is that Georges—or rather his instrument—was kept very busy, and that by the morning little of the recording material was left unused. For it seems that Hercule was indeed appropriately named. . . .

"When this piquant episode was finished, Georges had very little money left, but he did possess two recordings that were quite beyond price. Once more he set off to Paris, where, with practically no trouble, he came to terms with some businessmen who were so astonished that they gave him a very generous contract before coming to their senses. I am pleased to report this, because so often the scientist emerges second best in his dealings with the world of finance. I'm equally pleased to record that Georges had made provision for Professor Julian in the contract. You may say cynically that it was, after all, the Professor's invention, and that sooner or later Georges would have had to square him. But I like to think that there was more to it than that.

"The full details of the scheme for exploiting the device are, of course, unknown to me. I gather that Georges had been expansively eloquent—not that much eloquence was needed to convince anyone who had once experienced one or both of his play-backs. The market would be enormous, unlimited. The export trade alone could put France on her feet again and would wipe out her dollar deficit overnight—once certain snags had been overcome. Everything would have to be managed through somewhat clandestine channels, for think of the hub-bub from the hypocritical Anglo-saxons when they discovered just what was being imported into their countries. The Mother's Union, The Daughters of the American Revolution, The Housewives League, and *all* the religious organisations would rise as one. The lawyers were looking into the matter very carefully, and as far as could be seen the regulations that still excluded *Tropic of Capricorn* from the mails of the English-speaking countries could not be applied to this case—for the simple reason that no-one had thought of it. But there would be such a shout for new laws that Parliament and Congress would have to do something, so it was best to keep under cover as long as possible.

"In fact, as one of the directors pointed out, if the recordings were banned, so much the better. They could make much more money on a smaller output, because the price would promptly soar and all the vigilance of the Customs Officials couldn't block every leak. It would be Prohibition all over again.

"You will scarcely be surprised to hear that by this time Georges had somewhat lost interest in the gastronomical angle. It was an interesting but definitely minor possibility of the invention. Indeed, this had been tacitly admitted by the directors as they drew up the articles of association, for they had included the pleasures of the *cuisine* among 'subsidiary rights'.

"Georges returned home with his head in the clouds, and a substantial check in his pocket. A charming fancy had struck his imagination. He thought of all the trouble to which the gramophone companies had gone so that the world might have the complete recordings of the Forty-eight Preludes and Fugues or the Nine Symphonies. Well, *his* new company would put out a complete and definite set of recordings, performed by experts versed in the most esoteric knowledge of East and West. How many *opus* numbers would be required? That, of course, had been a subject of profound debate for some thousands of years. The Hindu text-books, Georges had heard, got well into three figures. It would be a most interesting research, combining profit with pleasure in an unexampled manner. . . . He had already begun some preliminary studies, using treatises which even in Paris were none too easy to obtain.

"If you think that while all this was going on, Georges had neglected his usual interests, you are all too right. He was working literally night and day, for he had not yet revealed his plans to the Professor and almost everything had to be done when the lab was closed. And one of the interests he had had to neglect was Yvonne.

"Her curiosity had already been aroused, as any girl's would have been. But now she was more than intrigued—she was distracted. For Georges had become so remote and cold. He was no longer in love with her.

"It was a result that might have been anticipated. Publicans have to guard against the danger of sampling their own wares too often—I'm sure *you* don't, Drew—and Georges had fallen into this seductive trap. He had been through that recording too many times, with somewhat debilitating results. Moreover, poor Yvonne was not to be compared with the experienced and talented Susette. It was the old story of the professional versus the amateur.

"All that Yvonne knew was that Georges was in love with someone else. That was true enough. She suspected that he had been unfaithful to her. And *that* raises profound philosophical questions we can hardly go into here.

"This being France, in case you had forgotten, the outcome was inevitable. Poor Georges! He was working late one night at the lab, as usual, when Yvonne finished him off with one of those ridiculous ornamental pistols which are *de rigeur* for such occasions. Let us drink to his memory."

"That's the trouble with all your stories," said John Beynon. "You tell us about wonderful inventions, and then at the end it turns out that the discoverer was killed, so no-one can do anything about it. For I suppose, as usual, the apparatus was destroyed?"

"But no," replied Purvis. "Apart from Georges, this is one of the stories that has a happy ending. There was no trouble at all about Yvonne, of course. Georges' grieving sponsors arrived on the scene with great speed and prevented any adverse publicity. Being men of sentiment as well as men of business, they realised that they would have to secure Yvonne's freedom. They promptly did this by playing the recording to *le Maire* and *le Préfet*, thus convincing them that the poor girl had experienced irresistible provocation. A few shares in the new company clinched the deal, with expressions of the utmost cordiality on both sides. Yvonne even got her gun back."

"Then when—" began someone else.

"Ah, these things take time. There's the question of mass production, you know. It's quite possible that distribution has already commenced through private—*very* private—channels. Some of those dubious little shops and notice boards around Leicester Square may soon start giving hints."

"Of course," said the New England voice disrespectfully, "you wouldn't know the *name* of the company."

You can't help admiring Purvis at times like this. He scarcely hesitated.

"*Le Société Anonyme d'Aphrodite*," he replied. "And I've just remembered something that will cheer *you* up. They hope to get round your sticky mails regulations and establish themselves before the inevitable congressional enquiry starts. They're opening up a branch in Nevada: apparently you can still get away with anything there." He raised his glass.

"To Georges Dupin," he said solemnly. "Martyr to science. Remember him when the fireworks start. And one other thing—"

"Yes?" we all asked.

"Better start saving now. And sell your TV sets before the bottom drops out of the market."

Armaments Race

As I've remarked on previous occasions, no-one has ever succeeded in pinning-down Harry Purvis, prize raconteur of the "White Hart," for any length of time. Of his scientific knowledge there can be no doubt—but where did he pick it up? And what justification is there for the terms of familiarity with which he speaks of so many Fellows of the Royal Society? There are, it must be admitted, many who do not believe a single word he says. That, I feel, is going a little too far, as I recently remarked somewhat forcibly to Bill Temple.

"You're always gunning for Harry," I said, "but you must admit that he provides entertainment. And that's more than most of us can say."

"If you're being personal," retorted Bill, still rankling over the fact that some perfectly serious stories had just been returned by an American editor on the grounds that they hadn't made him laugh, "step outside and say that again." He glanced through the window, noticed that it was still snowing hard, and hastily added, "not today, then, but maybe sometime in the summer, if we're both here on the Wednesday that catches it. Have another of your favourite shots of straight pineapple juice?"

"Thanks," I said. "One day I'll ask for a gin with it, just to shake you. I think I must be the only guy in the White Hart who can take it or leave it—*and* leaves it."

This was as far as the conversation got, because the subject of the discussion then arrived. Normally, this would merely have added fuel to the controversy, but as Harry had a stranger with him we decided to be polite little boys.

"Hello, folks," said Harry. "Meet my friend Solly Blumberg. Best special effects man in Hollywood."

"Let's be accurate, Harry," said Mr. Blumberg sadly, in a voice that should have belonged to a whipped spaniel. "Not *in* Hollywood. *Out* of Hollywood."

Harry waved the correction aside.

"All the better for you. Sol's come over here to apply his talents to the British film industry."

"There *is* a British film industry?" said Solly anxiously. "No-one seemed very sure round the studio."

"Sure there is. It's in a very flourishing condition, too. The Government piles on an entertainment tax that drives it to bankruptcy, then keeps it alive with whacking big grants. That's the way we do things in this country. Hey, Drew, where's the Visitor's Book? And a double for both of us. Solly's had a terrible time—he needs a bit of building up."

I cannot say that, apart from his hang-dog look, Mr. Blumberg had the appearance of a man who had suffered extreme hardships. He was neatly dressed in a Hart, Schaffner and Marx suit, and the points of his shirt collar buttoned down somewhere around the middle of his chest. That was thoughtful of them as they thus concealed something, but not enough, of his tie. I wondered what the trouble was. Not Un-American activities *again*, I prayed: that would trigger off our pet communist, who at the moment was peaceably studying a chess-board in the corner.

We all made sympathetic noises and John said rather pointedly: "Maybe it'll help to get it off your chest. It will be such a change to hear someone else talking around here."

"Don't be so modest, John," cut in Harry promptly. "*I'm* not tired of hearing you yet. But I doubt if Solly feels much like going through it again. Do you, old man?"

"No," said Mr. Blumberg. "*You* tell them."

("I knew it would come to that," sighed John in my ear.)

"Where shall I begin?" asked Harry. "The time Lillian Ross came to interview you?"

"Anywhere but *there*," shuddered Solly. "It really started when we were making the first 'Captain Zoom' serial."

" 'Captain Zoom'?" said someone ominously. "Those are two very rude words in this place. Don't say you were responsible for *that* unspeakable rubbish!"

"Now boys!" put in Harry in his best oil-on-troubled-waters voice. "Don't be too harsh. We can't apply our own high standards of criticism to everything. And people have got to earn a living. Besides, millions of kids *like* Captain Zoom. Surely you wouldn't want to break their little hearts—and so near Xmas, too!"

"If they *really* liked Captain Zoom, I'd rather break their little necks."

"Such unseasonable sentiments! I really must apologise for some of my compatriots, Solly. Let's see, what was the name of the first serial?"

" 'Captain Zoom and the Menace from Mars.' "

"Ah yes, that's right. Incidentally, I wonder why we always are menaced by Mars? I suppose that man Wells started it. One day we may have a big interplanetary libel action on our hands—unless we can prove that the Martians have been equally rude about *us*.

"I'm very glad to say that I never saw 'Menace From Mars.' ("I did," moaned somebody in the background. "I'm still trying to forget it.")—but we are not concerned with the story, such as it was. That was written by three men in a bar on Wilshire Boulevard. No-one is sure whether the Menace came out the way it did because the script writers were drunk, or whether they had to keep drunk in order to face the Menace. If that's confusing, don't bother. All that Solly was concerned with were the special effects that the director demanded.

"First of all, he had to build Mars. To do this he spent half an hour with 'The Conquest of Space,' and then emerged with a sketch which the carpenters turned into an over-ripe orange floating in nothingness, with an improbable number of stars around it. *That* was easy. The Martian cities weren't so simple. You try and think of *completely alien* architecture that still makes sense. I doubt if it's possible—if it will work at all, someone's already used it here on Earth. What the studio finally built was vaguely Byzantine with touches of Frank Lloyd Wright. The fact that none of the doors led anywhere didn't really matter, as long as there was enough room on the sets for the swordplay and general acrobatics that the script demanded.

"Yes—swordplay. Here was a civilisation which had atomic power, death-rays, spaceships, television and such-like modern conveniences, but when it came to a fight between Captain Zoom and the evil Emperor Klugg, the clock went back a couple of centuries. A lot of soldiers stood round holding deadly-looking ray-guns, but they never *did* anything with them. Well, hardly ever. Sometimes a shower of sparks would chase Captain Zoom and singe his pants, but that was all. I suppose that as the rays couldn't very well move faster than light, he could always outrun them.

"Still, those ornamental ray-guns gave everyone quite a few headaches. It's funny how Hollywood will spend endless trouble on some minute detail in a film which is complete rubbish. The director of Captain Zoom had a thing about ray-guns. Solly designed the Mark I, that looked like a cross between a bazooka and a blunder-bus. He was quite satisfied with it, and so was the director—for about a day. And then the great man came raging into the studio carrying a revolting creation of purple plastic with knobs and lenses and levers.

" 'Lookit this, Solly!' he puffed. 'Junior got it down at the Supermarket—they're being given away with packets of Crunch. Collect ten lids, and you get one. Hell, they're better than ours! And they *work*!'

"He pressed a lever, and a thin stream of water shot across the set and disappeared behind Captain Zoom's spaceship, where it promptly extinguished a cigaret that had no right to be burning there. An angry stage-hand emerged through the airlock, saw who it was had drenched him, and swiftly retreated, muttering things about his Union.

"Solly examined the ray-gun with annoyance and yet with an expert's discrimination. Yes, it was certainly much more impressive than anything *he'd* put out. He retired into his office and promised to see what he could do about it.

"The Mark II had everything built into it, including a television screen. If Captain Zoom was suddenly confronted by a charging hickoderm, all he had to do was to switch on the set, wait for the tubes to warm up, check the channel selector, adjust the fine tuning, touch up the focus, twiddle with the Line and Frame holds—and then press the trigger. He was, fortunately, a man of unbelievably swift reactions.

"The director was impressed, and the Mark II went into production. A slightly different model, the Mark IIa, was built for the Emperor Klugg's diabolical cohorts. It would never do, of course, if both sides had the same weapon. I told you that Pandemic Productions were sticklers for accuracy.

"All went well until the first rushes, and even beyond.

While the cast was acting, if you can use that word, they had to point the guns and press the triggers as if something was really happening. The sparks and flashes, however, were put on the negative later by two little men in a darkroom about as well guarded as Fort Knox. They did a good job, but after a while the producer again felt twinges in his overdeveloped artistic conscience.

" 'Solly,' he said, toying with the plastic horror which had reached Junior by courtesy of Crunch, the Succulent Cereal—Not a Burp in a Barrel—'Solly, I still want a gun that *does* something.'

"Solly ducked in time, so the jet went over his head and baptised a photograph of Louella Parsons.

" 'You're not going to start shooting all over again!" he wailed.

" 'Nooo,' replied the producer, with obvious reluctance. 'We'll have to use what we've got. But it *looks* faked, somehow.' He ruffled through the script on his desk, then brightened up.

" 'Now next week we start on Episode 54—"Slaves of the Slug-Men." Well, the Slug-Men gotta have guns, so what I'd like you to do is this—'

"The Mark III gave Solly a lot of trouble. (I haven't missed out one yet, have I? Good.) Not only had it to be a completely new design, but as you'll have gathered it had to 'do something'. This was a challenge to Solly's ingenuity: however, if I may borrow from Professor Toynbee, it was a challenge that evoked the appropriate response.

"Some high-powered engineering went into the Mark III. Luckily, Solly knew an ingenious technician who'd helped him out on similar occasions before, and he was really the man behind it. ('I'll say he was!' said Mr. Blumberg gloomily.) The principle was to use a jet of air, produced by a small but extremely powerful electric fan, and then to spray finely divided powder into it. When the thing was adjusted correctly, it shot out a most impressive beam, and made a still more impressive noise. The actors were so scared of it that their performances became most realistic.

"The producer was delighted—for a full three days. Then a dreadful doubt assailed him.

" 'Solly,' he said, 'Those damn guns are *too* good. The Slug-Men can beat the pants off Captain Zoom. We'll have to give him something better.'

"It was at this point that Solly realised what had happened. He had become involved in an armaments race.

"Let's see, this brings us to the Mark IV, doesn't it? How did *that* work?—oh yes, I remember. It was a glorified oxy-acetylene burner, with various chemicals injected into it to produce the most beautiful flames. I should have mentioned that from Episode 50—'Doom on Deimos'—the studio had switched over from black and white to Murkicolor, and great possibilities were thus opened up. By squirting copper or strontium or barium into the jet, you could get any colour you wanted.

"If you think that by this time the Producer was satisfied, you don't know Hollywood. Some cynics may still laugh when the motto 'Ars Gratia Artis' flashes on the screen, but this attitude, I submit, is not in accordance with the facts. Would such old fossils as Michaelangelo, Rembrandt or Titian have spent so much time, effort and money on the quest for perfection as did Pandemic Productions? I think not.

"I don't pretend to remember all the Marks that Solly and his ingenious engineer friend produced during the course of the serial. There was one that shot out a stream of coloured smoke-rings. There was the high-frequency generator that produced enormous but quite harmless sparks. There was a particularly ingenious *curved* beam produced by a jet of water with light reflected along inside it, which looked most spectacular in the dark. And finally, there was the Mark 12."

"Mark 13," said Mr. Blumberg.

"Of course—how stupid of me! What other number *could* it have been! The Mark 13 was not actually a portable weapon—though some of the others were portable only by a considerable stretch of the imagination. It was the diabolical device to be installed on Phobos in order to subjugate Earth. Though Solly has explained them to me once, the scientific principles involved escape my simple mind . . . However, who am I to match my brains against the intellects responsible for Captain Zoom? I can only report what the ray was supposed to do, not how it did it. It was to start a chain reaction in the atmosphere of our unfortunate planet, making the nitrogen and the oxygen in the air combine—with highly deleterious effects to terrestrial life.

"I'm not sure whether to be sorry or glad that Solly left all the details of the fabulous Mark 13 to his talented assistant. Though I've questioned him at some length, all he can tell me is that the thing was about six feet high and looked like a cross between the 200 inch telescope and an anti-aircraft gun. That's not very helpful, is it?

"He also says that there were a lot of radio tubes in the brute, as well as a thundering great magnet. And it was definitely supposed to produce a harmless but impressive electric arc, which could be distorted into all sorts of interesting shapes by the magnet. *That* was what the inventor said, and, despite everything, there is still no reason to disbelieve him.

"By one of those mischances that later turns out to be providential, Solly wasn't at the studio when they tried out the Mark 13. To his great annoyance, he had to be down in Mexico that day. And wasn't that lucky for you, Solly! He was expecting a long-distance call from one of his friends in the afternoon, but when it came through it wasn't the kind of message he'd anticipated.

"The Mark 13 had been, to put it mildly, a success. No-one knew exactly what had happened, but by a miracle no lives had been lost and the fire department had been able to save the adjoining studios. It was incredible, yet the facts were beyond dispute. The Mark 13 was supposed to be a phony death-ray—and it had turned out to be a real one. *Something* had emerged from the projector, and gone through the studio wall as if it wasn't there. Indeed, a moment later it wasn't. There was just a great big hole, beginning to smoulder round the edges. And then the roof fell in. . . .

"Unless Solly could convince the F.B.I. that it was all a mistake, he'd better stay the other side of the border. Even now the Pentagon and the Atomic Energy Commission were converging upon the wreckage. . . .

"What would you have done in Solly's shoes? He was innocent, but how could he prove it? Perhaps he would have gone back to face the music if he hadn't remembered that he'd once hired a man who'd campaigned for Henry Wallace, back in '48. *That* might take some explaining away: besides, Solly was a little tired of Captain Zoom. So here he is. Anyone know of a British film company that might have an opening for him? But historical films only, please. He won't touch anything more up-to-date than cross-bows."

Critical Mass

"Did I ever tell you," said Harry Purvis modestly, "about the time I prevented the evacuation of southern England?"

"You did not," said Charles Willis, "or if you did, I slept through it."

"Well, then," continued Harry, when enough people had gathered round him to make a respectable audience. "It happened two years ago at the Atomic Energy Research Establishment near Clobham. You all know the place, of course. But I don't think I've mentioned that I worked there for a while, on a special job I can't talk about."

"*That* makes a nice change," said John Wyndham, without the slightest effect.

"It was on a Saturday afternoon," Harry began. "A beautiful day in late spring. There were about six of us scientists in the bar of the "Black Swan," and the windows were open so that we could see down the slopes of Clobham Hill and out across the country to Upchester, about thirty miles away. It was so clear, in fact, that we could pick out the twin spires of Upchester Cathedral on the horizon. You couldn't have asked for a more peaceful day.

"The staff from the Establishment got on pretty well with the locals, though at first they weren't at all happy about having us on their doorsteps. Apart from the nature of our work, they'd believed that scientists were a race apart, with no human interests. When we'd beaten them up at darts a couple of times, and bought a few drinks, they changed their minds. But there was still a certain amount of half-serious leg-pulling, and we were always being asked what we were going to blow up next.

"On this afternoon there should have been several more of us present, but there'd been a rush job in the Radio-isotopes Division and so we were below strength. Stanley Chambers, the landlord, commented on the absence of some familiar faces.

" 'What's happened to all your pals today?' he asked my boss, Dr. French.

" 'They're busy at the works,' French replied—we always called the Establishment "the Works," as that made it seem more homely and less terrifying. 'We had to get some stuff out in a hurry. They'll be along later.'

" 'One day,' said Stan severely, 'you and your friends are going to let out something you won't be able to bottle up again. And *then* where will we all be?'

" 'Half-way to the Moon,' said Dr. French. I'm afraid it was rather an irresponsible sort of remark, but silly questions like this always made him lose patience.

"Stan Chambers looked over his shoulder as if he was judging how much of the hill stood between him and Clobham. I guessed he was calculating if he'd have time to reach the cellar—or whether it was worth trying anyway.

" 'About these—isotopes—you keep sending to the hospitals,' said a thoughtful voice. 'I was at St. Thomas' last week, and saw them moving some around in a lead safe that must have weighed a ton. It gave me the creeps, wondering what would happen if someone forgot to handle it properly.'

" 'We calculated the other day,' said Dr. French, obviously still annoyed at the interruption to his darts, 'that there was enough uranium in Clobham to boil the North Sea.'

"Now that was a silly thing to say: and it wasn't true, either. But I couldn't very well reprimand my own boss, could I?

"The man who'd been asking these questions was sitting in the alcove by the window, and I noticed that he was looking down the road with an anxious expression.

" 'The stuff leaves your place on trucks, doesn't it?' he asked, rather urgently.

" 'Yes: a lot of isotopes are short-lived, and so they've got to be delivered immediately.'

" 'Well, there's a truck in trouble down the hill. Would it be one of yours?'

"The dart-board was forgotten in the general rush to the window. When I managed to get a good look, I could see a large truck, loaded with packing cases, careering down the hill about a quarter of a mile away. From time to time it bounced off one of the hedges: it was obvious that the brakes had failed and the driver had lost control. Luckily there was no on-coming traffic, or a nasty accident would have been inevitable. As it was, one looked probable.

"Then the truck came to a bend in the road, left the pavement, and tore through the hedge. It rocked along with diminishing speed for fifty yards, jolting violently over the rough ground. It had almost come to rest when it encountered a ditch and, very sedately, canted over on to one side. A few seconds later the sound of splintering wood reached us as the packing cases slid off to the ground.

" 'That's that,' said someone with a sigh of relief. 'He did the right thing, aiming for the hedge. I guess he'll be shaken up, but he won't be hurt.'

"And then we saw a most perplexing sight. The door of the cab opened, and the driver scrambled out. Even from this distance, it was clear that he was highly agitated—though, in the circumstances, that was natural enough. But he did not, as one would have expected, sit down to recover his wits. On the contrary: he promptly took to his heels and ran across the field as if all the demons of hell were after him.

"We watched open-mouthed, and with rising apprehension, as he dwindled down the hill. There was an ominous silence in the bar, except for the ticking of the clock that Stan always kept exactly ten minutes fast. Then someone said, 'D'you think we'd better stay? I mean—it's only half a mile. . . .'

"There was an uncertain movement away from the window. Then Dr. French gave a nervous little laugh.

" 'We don't know if it *is* one of our trucks,' he said. 'And anyway, I was pulling your legs just now. It's completely impossible for any of this stuff to explode. He's just afraid his tank's going to catch fire.'

" 'Oh yes?' said Stan. 'Then why's he still running? He's half-way down the hill now.'

" 'I know!" suggested Charlie Evan, from the Instruments Section. 'He's carrying explosives, and is afraid they're going to go up.'

"I had to scotch that one. 'There's no sign of a fire, so what's he worried about now? And if he *was* carrying explosives, he'd have a red flag or something.'

" 'Hang on a minute,' said Stan. 'I'll go and get my glasses.'

"No one moved until he came back: no one, that is, except the tiny figure far down the hill-side, which had now vanished into the woods without slackening its speed.

"Stan stared through the binoculars for an eternity. At last he lowered them with a grunt of disappointment.

" 'Can't see much,' he said. 'The truck's tipped over in the wrong direction. Those crates are all over the place—some of them have busted open. See if you can make anything of it.'

"French had a long stare, then handed the glasses to me.

They were a very old-fashioned model, and didn't help much. For a moment it seemed to me that there was a curious haziness about some of the boxes—but that didn't make sense. I put it down to the poor condition of the lenses.

"And there, I think, the whole business would have fizzled out if those cyclists hadn't appeared. They were puffing up the hill on a tandem, and when they came to the fresh gap in the hedge they promptly dismounted to see what was going on. The truck was visible from the road and they approached it hand in hand, the girl obviously hanging back, the man telling her not to be nervous. We could imagine their conversation: it was a most touching spectacle.

"It didn't last long. They got to within a few yards of the truck—and then departed at high speed in opposite directions. Neither looked back to observe the other's progress; and they were running, I noticed, in a most peculiar fashion.

"Stan, who'd retrieved his glasses, put them down with a shaky hand.

" 'Get out the cars!' he said.

" 'But—' began Dr. French.

"Stan silenced him with a glare. 'You damned scientists!' he said, as he slammed and locked the till (even at a moment like this, he remembered his duty). 'I knew you'd do it sooner or later.'

"Then he was gone, and most of his cronies with him. They didn't stop to offer us a lift.

" 'This is perfectly ridiculous!' said French. 'Before we know where we are, those fools will have started a panic and there'll be hell to pay.'

"I knew what he meant. Someone would tell the police: cars would be diverted away from Clobham: the telephone lines would be blocked with calls—it would be like the Orson Welles 'War of the Worlds' scare back in 1938. Perhaps you think I'm exaggerating, but you can never underestimate the power of panic. And people were scared, remember, of our place, and were half-expecting something like this to happen.

"What's more, I don't mind telling you that by this time we weren't any too happy ourselves. We were simply unable to imagine what was going on down there by the wrecked truck, and there's nothing a scientist hates more than being completely baffled.

"Meanwhile I'd grabbed Stan's discarded binoculars and had been studying the wreck very carefully. As I looked, a theory began to evolve in my mind. There *was* some—aura—about those boxes. I stared until my eyes began to smart, and then said to Dr. French: 'I think I know what it is. Suppose you ring up Clobham Post Office and try to intercept Stan, or at least to stop him spreading rumours if he's already got there. Say that everything's under control—there's nothing to worry about. While you're doing that, I'm going to walk down to the truck and test my theory.'

"I'm sorry to say that no one offered to follow me. Though I started down the road confidently enough, after a while I began to be a little less sure of myself. I remembered an incident that's always struck me as one of history's most ironic jokes, and began to wonder if something of the same sort might not be happening now. There was once a volcanic island in the Far East, with a population of about 50,000. No one worried about the volcano, which had been quiet for a hundred years. Then, one day, eruptions started. At first they were minor, but they grew more intense hour by hour. The people started to panic, and tried to crowd aboard the few boats in harbour so that they could reach the mainland.

"But the island was ruled by a military commandant who was determined to keep order at all costs. He sent out proclamations saying that there was no danger, and he got his troops to occupy the ships so that there would be no loss of life as people attempted to leave in overloaded boats. Such was the force of his personality, and the example of his courage, that he calmed the multitude, and those who had been trying to get away crept shame-faced back to their homes, where they sat waiting for conditions to return to normal.

"So when the volcano blew up a couple of hours later, taking the whole island with it, there weren't any survivors at all. . . .

"As I got near the truck, I began to see myself in the role of that misguided commandant. After all, there are some times when it is brave to stay and face danger, and others when the most sensible thing to do is to take to the hills. But it was too late to turn back now, and *I* was fairly sure of my theory."

"I know," said George Whiteley, who always liked to spoil Harry's stories if he could. "It was gas."

Harry didn't seem at all perturbed at losing his climax.

"Ingenious of you to suggest it. That's just what I did think, which shows that we can all be stupid at times.

"I'd got to within fifty feet of the truck when I stopped dead, and though it was a warm day a most unpleasant chill began to spread out from the small of my back. For I could see something that blew my gas theory to blazes and left nothing at all in its place.

"A black, crawling mass was writhing over the surface of one of the packing cases. For a moment I tried to pretend to myself that it was some dark liquid oozing from a broken container. But one rather well-known characteristic of liquids is that they can't defy gravity. This thing was doing just that: and it was also quite obviously alive. From where I was standing, it looked like the pseudopod of some giant amoeba as it changed its shape and thickness, and wavered to and fro over the side of the broken crate.

"Quite a few fantasies that would have done credit to Edgar

Allan Poe flitted through my mind in those few seconds. Then I remembered my duty as a citizen and my pride as a scientist: I started to walk forward again, though in no great haste.

"I remember sniffing cautiously, as if I still had gas on the mind. Yet it was my ears, not my nose, that gave me the answer, as the sound from that sinister, seething mass built up around me. It was a sound I'd heard a million times before, but never as loud as this. And I sat down—not too close—and laughed and laughed and laughed. Then I got up and walked back to the pub.

" 'Well,' said Dr. French eagerly, 'what is it? We've got Stan on the line—caught him at the crossroads. But he won't come back until we can tell him what's happening.'

" 'Tell Stan,' I said, 'to rustle up the local apiarist, and bring him along at the same time. There's a big job for him here.'

" 'The local *what*?' said French. Then his jaw dropped. 'My God! You don't mean. . . .'

" 'Precisely,' I answered, walking behind the bar to see if Stan had any interesting bottles hidden away. 'They're settling down now, but I guess they're still pretty annoyed. I didn't stop to count, but there must be half a million bees down there trying to get back into their busted hives.' "

The Ultimate Melody

Have you ever noticed that, when there are twenty or thirty people talking together in a room, there are occasional moments when everyone becomes suddenly silent, so that for a second there's a sudden, vibrating emptiness that seems to swallow up all sound? I don't know how it affects other people, but when it happens it makes me feel cold all over. Of course, the whole thing's merely caused by the laws of probability, but somehow it seems more than a mere coinciding of conversational pauses. It's almost as if everybody is listening for something—they don't know what. At such moments I say to myself:

> *But at my back I always hear*
> *Time's wingéd chariot hurrying near. . . .*

That's how *I* feel about it, however cheerful the company in which it happens. Yes, even if it's in the "White Hart."

It was like that one Wednesday evening when the place wasn't quite as crowded as usual. The Silence came, as unexpectedly as it always does. Then, probably in a deliberate attempt to break that unsettling feeling of suspense, Charlie Willis started whistling the latest hit tune. I don't even remember what it was. I only remember that it triggered off one of Harry Purvis' most disturbing stories.

"Charlie," he began, quietly enough. "That darn tune's driving me mad. I've heard it every time I've switched on the radio for the last week."

There was a sniff from John Christopher.

"You ought to stay tuned to the Third Programme. Then you'd be safe."

"Some of us," retorted Harry, "don't care for an exclusive diet of Elizabethan madrigals. But don't let's quarrel about *that*, for heaven's sake. Has it ever occurred to you that there's something rather—*fundamental*—about hit tunes?"

"What do you mean?"

"Well, they come along out of nowhere, and then for weeks everybody's humming them, just as Charlie did then. The good ones grab hold of you so thoroughly that you just can't get them out of your head—they go round and round for days. And then, suddenly, they've vanished again."

"I know what you mean," said Art Vincent. "There are some melodies that you can take or leave, but others stick like treacle, whether you want them or not."

"Precisely. I got saddled that way for a whole week with the big theme from the finale of Sibelius Two—even went to sleep with it running round inside my head. Then there's that 'Third Man' piece—da di da di *daa*, di da, di *daa* . . . look what *that* did to everybody."

Harry had to pause for a moment until his audience had stopped zithering. When the last "Plonk!" had died away he continued:

"Precisely! You all felt the same way. Now what *is* there about these tunes that has this effect? Some of them are great music—others just banal, but they've obviously got *something* in common."

"Go on," said Charlie. "We're waiting."

"I don't know what the answer is," replied Harry. "And what's more, I don't want to. For I know a man who found out."

Automatically, someone handed him a beer, so that the tenor of his tale would not be disturbed. It always annoyed a lot of people when he had to stop in mid-flight for a refill.

"I don't know why it is," said Harry Purvis, "that most scientists are interested in music, but it's an undeniable fact. I've known several large labs that had their own amateur symphony orchestras—some of them quite good, too. As far as the mathematicians are concerned, one can think of obvious reasons for this fondness: music, particularly classical music, has a form which is almost mathematical. And then, of course, there's the underlying theory—harmonic relations, wave analysis, frequency distribution, and so on. It's a fascinating study in itself, and one that appeals strongly to the scientific mind. Moreover, it doesn't—as some people might think—preclude a purely aesthetic appreciation of music for its own sake.

"However, I must confess that Gilbert Lister's interest in music was purely cerebral. He was, primarily, a physiologist, specialising in the study of the brain. So when I said that his interest was cerebral, I meant it quite literally. 'Alexander's Ragtime Band' and the Choral Symphony were all the same to him. He wasn't concerned with the sounds themselves, but only what happened when they got past the ears and started doing things to the brain.

"In an audience as well educated as this," said Harry, with an emphasis that made it sound positively insulting, "there will be no-one who's unaware of the fact that much of the brain's activity is electrical. There are, in fact, steady pulsing rhythms going on all the time, and they can be detected and analysed by modern instruments. This was Gilbert Lister's line of territory. He could stick electrodes on your scalp and his amplifiers would draw your brainwaves on yards of tape. Then he could examine them and tell you all sorts of interesting things about yourself. Ultimately, he claimed, it would be possible to identify anyone from their encephalogram—to use the correct term—more positively than by fingerprints. A man might get a surgeon to change his skin, but if we ever got to the stage when surgery could change your brain—well, you'd have turned into somebody else, anyway, so the system still wouldn't have failed.

"It was while he was studying the alpha, beta and other rhythms in the brain that Gilbert got interested in music. He was sure that there must be some connexion between musical and mental rhythms. He'd play music at various tempos to his subjects and see what effect it had on their normal brain frequencies. As you might expect, it had a lot, and the discoveries he made led Gilbert on into more philosophical fields.

"I only had one good talk with him about his theories. It was not that he was at all secretive—I've never met a scientist who was, come to think of it—but he didn't like to talk about his work until he knew where it was leading. However, what he told me was enough to prove that he'd opened up a very interesting line of territory, and thereafter I made rather a point of cultivating him. My firm supplied some of his equipment, but I wasn't averse to picking up a little profit on the side. It occurred to me that *if* Gilbert's ideas worked out, he'd need a business manager before you could whistle the opening bar of the Fifth Symphony. . . .

"For what Gilbert was trying to do was to lay a scientific foundation for the theory of hit-tunes. Of course, he didn't think of it that way: he regarded it as a pure research project, and didn't look any further ahead than a paper in the *Proceed-*

ings of the Physical Society. But I spotted its financial implications at once. They were quite breath-taking.

"Gilbert was sure that a great melody, or a hit tune, made its impression on the mind because in some way it fitted in with the fundamental electrical rhythms going on in the brain. One analogy he used was 'It's like a Yale key going into a lock—the two patterns have got to fit before anything happens.'

"He tackled the problem from two angles. In the first place, he took hundreds of the really famous tunes in classical and popular music and analysed their structure—their morphology, as he put it. This was done automatically, in a big harmonic analyser that sorted out all the frequencies. Of course, there was a lot more to it than this, but I'm sure you've got the basic idea.

"At the same time, he tried to see how the resulting patterns of waves agreed with the natural electrical vibrations of the brain. Because it was Gilbert's theory—and this is where we get into rather deep philosophical waters—that all existing tunes were merely crude approximations to one fundamental melody. Musicians had been groping for it down the centuries, but they didn't know what they were doing, because they were ignorant of the relation between music and mind. Now that this had been unravelled, it should be possible to discover the Ultimate Melody."

"Huh!" said John Christopher. "It's only a rehash of Plato's theory of ideals. You know—all the objects of our material world are merely crude copies of the ideal chair or table or what-have-you. So your friend was after the ideal melody. And did he find it?"

"I'll tell you," continued Harry imperturbably. "It took Gilbert about a year to complete his analysis, and then he started on the synthesis. To put it crudely, he built a machine that would automatically construct patterns of sound according to the laws that he'd uncovered. He had banks of oscillators and mixers—in fact, he modified an ordinary electronic organ for this part of the apparatus—which were controlled by his composing machine. In the rather childish way that scientists like to name their offspring, Gilbert had called this device Ludwig.

"Maybe it helps to understand how Ludwig operated if you think of him as a kind of kaleidoscope, working with sound rather than light. But he was a kaleidoscope set to obey certain laws, and those laws—so Gilbert believed—were based on the fundamental structure of the human mind. If he could get the adjustments correct, Ludwig would be bound, sooner or later, to arrive at the Ultimate Melody as he searched through all the possible patterns of music.

"I had one opportunity of hearing Ludwig at work, and it was uncanny. The equipment was the usual nondescript mess of electronics which one meets in any lab: it might have been a mock-up of a new computer, a radar gun-sight, a traffic control system, or a ham radio. It was very hard to believe that, if it worked, it would put every composer in the world out of business. Or would it? Perhaps not: Ludwig might be able to deliver the raw material, but surely it would still have to be orchestrated.

"Then the sound started to come from the speaker. At first it seemed to me that I was listening to the five-finger exercises of an accurate but completely uninspired pupil. Most of the themes were quite banal: the machine would play one, then ring the changes on it bar after bar until it had exhausted all the possibilities before going on to the next. Occasionally a quite striking phrase would come up, but on the whole I was not at all impressed.

"However, Gilbert explained that this was only a trial run and that the main circuits had not yet been set up. When they were, Ludwig would be far more selective: at the moment, he was playing everything that came along—he had no sense of discrimination. When he had acquired that, *then* the possibilities were limitless.

"That was the last time I ever saw Gilbert Lister. I had arranged to meet him at the lab about a week later, when he expected to have made substantial progress. As it happened, I was about an hour late for my appointment. And that was very lucky for me. . . .

"When I got there, they had just taken Gilbert away. His lab assistant, an old man who'd been with him for years, was sitting distraught and disconsolate among the tangled wiring of Ludwig. It took me a long time to discover what had happened, and longer still to work out the explanation.

"There was no doubt of one thing. Ludwig had finally worked. The assistant had gone off to lunch while Gilbert was making the final adjustments, and when he came back an hour later the laboratory was pulsing with one long and very complex melodic phrase. Either the machine had stopped automatically at that point, or Gilbert had switched it over to REPEAT. At any rate, he had been listening, for several hundred times at least, to that same melody. When his assistant found him, he seemed to be in a trance. His eyes were open yet unseeing, his limbs rigid. Even when Ludwig was switched off, it made no difference. Gilbert was beyond help.

"What had happened? Well, I suppose we should have thought of it, but it's so easy to be wise after the event. It's just as I said at the beginning. If a composer, working merely by rule of thumb, can produce a melody which can dominate your mind for days on end, imagine the effect of the Ultimate Melody for which Gilbert was searching! Supposing it existed—and I'm not admitting that it does—it would form an endless ring in the memory circuits of the mind. It would go round and round forever, obliterating all other thoughts. All the cloying melodies of the past would be mere ephemerae compared to it. Once it had keyed into the brain, and distorted the circling waveforms which are the physical manifestations of consciousness itself—that would be the end. And that is what happened to Gilbert.

"They've tried shock therapy—everything. But it's no good; the pattern has been set, and it can't be broken. He's lost all consciousness of the outer world, and has to be fed intravenously. He never moves or reacts to external stimuli, but sometimes, they tell me, he twitches in a peculiar way as if he is beating time. . . .

"I'm afraid there's no hope for him. Yet I'm not sure if his fate is a horrible one, or whether he should be envied. Perhaps, in a sense, he's found the ultimate reality that philosophers like Plato are always talking about. I really don't know. And sometimes I find myself wondering just what that infernal melody *was* like, and almost wishing that I'd been able to hear it perhaps once. There might have been some way of doing it in safety: remember how Ulysses listened to the song of the sirens and got away with it . . . ? But there'll never be a chance now, of course."

"I was waiting for this," said Charles Willis nastily. "I suppose the apparatus blew up, or something, so that as usual there's no way of checking your story."

Harry gave him his best more-in-sorrow-than-in-anger look.

"The apparatus was quite undamaged," he said severely. "What happened next was one of those completely maddening things for which I shall never stop blaming myself. You see, I'd been too interested in Gilbert's experiment to look after my firm's business in the way that I should. I'm afraid he'd fallen badly behind with his payments, and when the Accounts Department discovered what had happened to him they acted quickly. I was only off for a couple of days on another job, and when I got back, do you know what had happened? They'd pushed through a court order, and had seized all their property. Of course that had meant dismantling Ludwig: when I saw him next he was just a pile of useless junk. And all because of a few pounds! It made me weep."

"I'm sure of it," said Eric Maine. "But you've forgotten Loose End Number Two. *What about Gilbert's assistant?* He went into the lab while the gadget was going full blast. Why didn't it get him, too? You've slipped up here, Harry."

H. Purvis, Esquire, paused only to drain the last drops from his glass and to hand it silently across to Drew.

"Really!" he said. "Is this a cross-examination? I didn't mention the point because it was rather trivial. But it explains why I was never able to get the slightest inkling of the nature of that melody. You see, Gilbert's assistant was a first-rate lab technician, but he'd never been able to help much with the adjustments to Ludwig. For he was one of those people who are completely tone-deaf. To him, the Ultimate Melody meant no more than a couple of cats on a garden wall."

Nobody asked any more questions: we all, I think, felt the desire to commune with our thoughts. There was a long, brooding silence before the "White Hart" resumed its usual activities. And even then, I noticed, it was every bit of ten minutes before Charlie started whistling "La Ronde" again.

The Pacifist

I got to the "White Hart" late that evening, and when I arrived everyone was crowded into the corner under the dartboard. All except Drew, that is: he had not deserted his post, but was sitting behind the bar reading the collected T. S. Eliot. He broke off from "The Confidential Clerk" long enough to hand me a beer and to tell me what was going on.

"Eric's brought in some kind of games machine—it's beaten everybody so far. Sam's trying his luck with it now."

At that moment a roar of laughter announced that Sam had been no luckier than the rest, and I pushed my way through the crowd to see what was happening.

On the table lay a flat metal box the size of a checker-board, and divided into squares in a similar way. At the corner of each square was a two-way switch and a little neon lamp: the whole affair was plugged into the light socket (thus plunging the dartboard into darkness) and Eric Rodgers was looking round for a new victim.

"What does the thing do?" I asked.

"It's a modification of naughts and crosses—what the

Americans call Tic-Tac-Toe. Shannon showed it to me when I was over at Bell Labs. What you have to do is to complete a path from one side of the board to the other—call it North to South—by turning these switches. Imagine the thing forms a grid of streets, if you like, and these neons are the traffic lights. You and the machine take turns making moves. The machine tries to block your path by building one of its own in the East-West direction—the little neons light up to tell you which way it wants to make a move. Neither track need be a straight line: you can zig-zag as much as you like. All that matters is that the path must be continuous, and the one to get across the board first wins."

"Meaning the machine, I suppose?"

"Well, it's never been beaten yet."

"Can't you force a draw, by blocking the machine's path, so that at least you don't lose?"

"That's what we're trying: like to have a go?"

Two minutes later I joined the other unsuccessful contestants. The machine had dodged all my barriers and established its own track from East to West. I wasn't convinced that it was unbeatable, but the game was clearly a good deal more complicated than it looked.

Eric glanced round his audience when I had retired. No-one else seemed in a hurry to move forward.

"Ha!" he said. "The very man. What about you, Purvis? You've not had a shot yet."

Harry Purvis was standing at the back of the crowd, with a far-away look in his eye. He jolted back to earth as Eric addressed him, but didn't answer the question directly.

"Fascinating things, these electronic computers," he mused. "I suppose I shouldn't tell you this, but your gadget reminds me of what happened to Project Clausewitz. A curious story, and one very expensive to the American taxpayer."

"Look," said John Wyndham anxiously. "Before you start, be a good sport and let us get our glasses filled. Drew!"

This important matter having been attended to, we gathered round Harry. Only Charlie Willis still remained with the machine, hopefully trying his luck.

"As you all know," began Harry, "Science with a capital S is a big thing in the military world these days. The weapons side—rockets, atom bombs and so on—is only part of it, though that's all the public knows about. Much more fascinating, in my opinion, is the operational research angle. You might say that's concerned with brains rather than brute force. I once heard it defined as how to win wars without actually fighting, and that's not a bad description.

"Now you all know about the big electronic computers that cropped up like mushrooms in the 1950's. Most of them were built to deal with mathematical problems, but when you think about it you'll realise that War itself is a mathematical problem. It's such a complicated one that human brains can't handle it—there are far too many variables. Even the greatest strategist cannot see the picture as a whole: the Hitlers and Napoleons always make a mistake in the end.

"But a machine—that would be a different matter. A number of bright people realised this after the end of the war. The techniques that had been worked out in the building of ENIAC and the other big computers could revolutionize strategy.

"Hence Project Clausewitz. Don't ask me how I got to know about it, or press me for too many details. All that matters is that a good many megabucks worth of electronic equipment, and some of the best scientific brains in the United States, went into a certain cavern in the Kentucky hills. They're still there, but things haven't turned out exactly as they expected.

"Now I don't know what experience you have of high-ranking military officers, but there's one type you've all come across in fiction. That's the pompous, conservative, stick-in-the-mud careerist who's got to the top by sheer pressure from beneath, who does everything by rules and regulations and regards civilians as, at the best, unfriendly neutrals. I'll let you into a secret: he actually exists. He's not very common nowadays, but he's still around and sometimes it's not possible to find a safe job for him. When that happens, he's worth his weight in plutonium to the Other Side.

"Such a character, it seems, was General Smith. No, of *course* that wasn't his real name! His father was a Senator, and although lots of people in the Pentagon had tried hard enough, the old man's influence had prevented the General from being put in charge of something harmless, like the coast defence of Wyoming. Instead, by miraculous misfortune, he had been made the officer responsible for Project Clausewitz.

"Of course, he was only concerned with the administrative, not the scientific, aspects of the work. All might yet have been well had the General been content to let the scientists get on with their work while he concentrated on saluting smartness, the coefficient of reflection of barrack floors, and similar matters of military importance. Unfortunately, he didn't.

"The General had led a sheltered existence. He had, if I may borrow from Wilde (everybody else does) been a man of peace, except in his domestic life. He had never met scientists before, and the shock was considerable. So perhaps it is not fair to blame him for everything that happened.

"It was a considerable time before he realised the aims and objects of Project Clausewitz, and when he did he was quite disturbed. This may have made him feel even less friendly towards his scientific staff, for despite anything I may have said the General was not entirely a fool. He was intelligent enough to understand that, if the Project succeeded, there might be more ex-generals around than even the combined boards of management of American industry could comfortably absorb.

"But let's leave the General for a minute and have a look at the scientists. There were about fifty of them, as well as a couple of hundred technicians. They'd all been carefully screened by the F.B.I., so probably not more than half a dozen were active members of the Communist Party. Though there was a lot of talk of sabotage later, for once in a while the comrades were completely innocent. Besides, what happened certainly wasn't sabotage in any generally accepted meaning of the word. . . .

"The man who had really designed the computer was a quiet little mathematical genius who had been swept out of college into the Kentucky hills and the world of Security and Priorities before he'd really realised what had happened. He wasn't called Dr. Milquetoast, but he should have been and that's what I'll christen him.

"To complete our cast of characters, I'd better say something about Karl. At this stage in the business, Karl was only half-built. Like all big computers, most of him consisted of vast banks of memory units which could receive and store information until it was needed. The creative part of Karl's brain—the analysers and integrators—took this information and operated on it, to produce answers to the questions he was asked. Given all the relevant facts, Karl would produce the right answers. The problem, of course, was to see that Karl *did* have all the facts—he couldn't be expected to get the right results from inaccurate or insufficient information.

"It was Dr. Milquetoast's responsibility to design Karl's brain. Yes, I know that's a crudely anthropomorphic way of looking at it, but no-one can deny that these big computers have personalities. It's hard to put it more accurately without getting technical, so I'll simply say that little Milquetoast had to create the extremely complex circuits that enabled Karl to think in the way he was supposed to do.

"So here are our three protagonists—General Smith, pining for the days of Custer; Dr. Milquetoast, lost in the fascinating scientific intricasies of his job; and Karl, fifty tons of electronic gear, not yet animated by the currents that would soon be coursing through him.

"Soon—but not soon enough for General Smith. Let's not be too hard on the General: someone had probably put the pressure on him, when it became obvious that the Project was falling behind schedule. He called Dr. Milquetoast into his office.

"The interview lasted more than thirty minutes, and the doctor said less than thirty words. Most of the time the General was making pointed remarks about production times, deadlines and bottlenecks. He seemed to be under the impression that building Karl differed in no important particular from the assembly of the current model Ford: it was just a question of putting the bits together. Dr. Milquetoast was not the sort of man to explain the error, even if the General had given him the opportunity. He left, smarting under a considerable sense of injustice.

"A week later, it was obvious that the creation of Karl was falling still further behind schedule. Milquetoast was doing his best, and there was no-one who could do better. Problems of a complexity totally beyond the General's comprehension had to be met and mastered. They *were* mastered, but it took time, and time was in short supply.

"At his first interview, the General had tried to be as nice as he could, and had succeeded in being merely rude. This time, he tried to be rude, with results that I leave to your imagination. He practically insinuated that Milquetoast and his colleagues, by falling behind their deadlines, were guilty of un-American inactivity.

"From this moment onwards, two things started to happen. Relations between the Army and the scientists grew steadily worse; and Dr. Milquetoast, for the first time, began to give serious thought to the wider implications of his work. He had always been too busy, too engaged upon the immediate problems of his task, to consider his social responsibilities. He was still too busy now, but that didn't stop him pausing for reflection. "Here am I," he told himself, "one of the best pure mathematicians in the world—and what am I doing? What's happened to my thesis on Diophantine equations? When am I going to have another smack at the prime number theorem? In short, when am I going to do some *real* work again?"

"He could have resigned, but that didn't occur to him. In any case, far down beneath that mild and diffident exterior was a stubborn streak. Dr. Milquetoast continued to work, even more energetically than before. The construction of Karl proceeded slowly but steadily: the final connexions in his myriad-celled brain were soldered: the thousands of circuits were checked and tested by the mechanics.

"And one circuit, indistinguishably interwoven among its multitude of companions and leading to a set of memory cells apparently identical with all the others, was tested by Dr. Milquetoast alone, for no-one else knew that it existed.

"The great day came. To Kentucky, by devious routes, came very important personages. A whole constellation of multi-starred generals arrived from the Pentagon. Even the Navy had been invited.

"Proudly, General Smith led the visitors from cavern to cavern, from memory banks to selector networks to matrix analysers to input tables—and finally to the rows of electric typewriters on which Karl would print the results of his deliberations. The General knew his way around quite well: at least, he got most of the names right. He even managed to give the impression, to those who knew no better, that he was largely responsible for Karl.

" 'Now,' said the General cheerfully. 'Let's give him some work to do. Anyone like to set him a few sums?'

"At the word 'sums' the mathematicians winced, but the General was unaware of his *faux pas*. The assembled brass thought for a while: then someone said daringly, 'What's 9 multiplied by itself twenty times?'

"One of the technicians, with an audible sniff, punched a few keys. There was a rattle of gunfire from an electric typewriter, and before anyone could blink twice the answer had appeared—all twenty digits of it."

(I've looked it up since: for anyone who wants to know it's:—

12157665459056928801

But let's get back to Harry and his tale.)

"For the next fifteen minutes Karl was bombarded with similar trivialities. The visitors were impressed, though there was no reason to suppose that they'd have spotted it if all the answers had been completely wrong.

"The General gave a modest cough. Simple arithmetic was as far as he could go, and Karl had barely begun to warm up. 'I'll now hand you over,' he said, 'to Captain Winkler.'

"Captain Winkler was an intense young Harvard graduate whom the General distrusted, rightly suspecting him to be more a scientist than a military man. But he was the only officer who really understood what Karl was supposed to do, or could explain exactly how he set about doing it. He looked, the General thought grumpily, like a damned schoolmaster as he started to lecture the visitors.

"The tactical problem that had been set up was a complicated one, but the answer was already known to everybody except Karl. It was a battle that had been fought and finished almost a century before, and when Captain Winkler concluded his introduction, a general from Boston whispered to his aide, 'I'll bet some damn Southerner has fixed it so that Lee wins this time.' Everyone had to admit, however, that the problem was an excellent way of testing Karl's capabilities.

"The punched tapes disappeared into the capacious memory units: patterns of lights flickered and flashed across the registers; mysterious things happened in all directions.

" 'This problem,' said Captain Winkler primly, 'will take about five minutes to evaluate.'

"As if in deliberate contradiction, one of the typewriters promptly started to chatter. A strip of paper shot out of the feed, and Captain Winkler, looking rather puzzled at Karl's unexpected alacrity, read the message. His lower jaw immediately dropped six inches, and he stood staring at the paper as if unable to believe his eyes.

" 'What is it, man?' barked the General.

"Captain Winkler swallowed hard, but appeared to have lost the power of speech. With a snort of impatience, the General snatched the paper from him. Then it was his turn to stand paralysed, but unlike his subordinate he also turned a most beautiful red. For a moment he looked like some tropical fish strangling out of water: then, not without a slight scuffle, the enigmatic message was captured by the five-star general who outranked everybody in the room.

"His reaction was totally different. He promptly doubled up with laughter.

"The minor officers were left in a state of infuriating suspense for quite ten minutes. But finally the news filtered down through Colonels to Captains to Lieutenants, until at last there wasn't a G.I. in the establishment who did not know the wonderful news.

"Karl had told General Smith that he was a pompous baboon. That was all.

"Even though everybody agreed with Karl, the matter could

hardly be allowed to rest there. Something, obviously, had gone wrong. Something—or someone—had diverted Karl's attention from the Battle of Gettysburg.

'Where,' roared General Smith, finally recovering his voice, 'is Dr. Milquetoast?'

"He was no longer present. He had slipped quietly out of the room, having witnessed his great moment. Retribution would come later, of course, but it was worth it.

"The frantic technicians cleared the circuits and started running tests. They gave Karl an elaborate series of multiplications and divisions to perform—the computer's equivalent of 'The quick brown fox jumps over the lazy dog.' Everything seemed to be functioning perfectly. So they put in a very simple tactical problem, which a Lieutenant J. G. could solve in his sleep.

"Said Karl: 'Go jump in a lake, General.'

"It was then that General Smith realised that he was confronted with something outside the scope of Standard Operating Procedure. He was faced with mechanical mutiny, no less.

"It took several hours of tests to discover exactly what had happened. Somewhere tucked away in Karl's capacious memory units was a superb collection of insults, lovingly assembled by Dr. Milquetoast. He had punched on tape, or recorded in patterns of electrical impulses, everything he would like to have said to the General himself. But that was not all he had done: that would have been too easy, not worthy of his genius. He had also installed what could only be called a censor circuit—he had given Karl the power of discrimination. Before solving it, Karl examined every problem fed to him. If it was concerned with pure mathematics, he co-operated and dealt with it properly. But if it was a military problem—out came one of the insults. After twenty times, he had not repeated himself once, and the WAC's had already had to be sent out of the room.

"It must be confessed that after a while the technicians were almost as interested in discovering what indignity Karl would next heap upon General Smith as they were in finding the fault in the circuits. He had begun with mere insults and surprising genealogical surmises, but had swiftly passed on to detailed instructions the mildest of which would have been highly prejudicial to the General's dignity, while the more imaginative would have seriously imperilled his physical integrity. The fact that all these messages, as they emerged from the typewriters, were immediately classified TOP SECRET was small consolation to the recipient. He knew with a glum certainty that this would be the worst-kept secret of the cold war, and that it was time he looked round for a civilian occupation.

"And there, gentlemen," concluded Purvis, "the situation remains. The engineers are still trying to unravel the circuits that Dr. Milquetoast installed, and no doubt it's only a matter of time before they succeed. But meanwhile Karl remains an unyielding pacifist. He's perfectly happy playing with the theory of numbers, computing tables of powers, and handling arithmetical problems generally. Do you remember the famous toast 'Here's to pure mathematics—may it never be of any use to anybody'? Karl would have seconded that. . . .

"As soon as anyone attempts to slip a fast one across him, he goes on strike. And because he's got such a wonderful memory, he can't be fooled. He has half the great battles of the world stored up in his circuits, and can recognise at once any variations on them. Though attempts were made to disguise tactical exercises as problems in mathematics, he could spot the subterfuge right away. And out would come another *billet doux* for the General.

As for Dr. Milquetoast, no one could do much about him because he promptly had a nervous breakdown. It was suspiciously well timed, but he could certainly claim to have earned it. When last heard of he was teaching matrix algebra at a theological college in Denver. He swears he's forgotten everything that had ever happened while he was working on Karl. Maybe he was even telling the truth. . . ."

There was a sudden shout from the back of the room.

"I've won!" cried Charles Willis. "Come and see!"

We all crowded under the dartboard. It seemed true enough. Charlie had established a zig-zag but continuous track from one side of the checker-board to the other, despite the obstacles the machine had tried to put in his way.

"Show us how you did it," said Eric Rodgers.

Charlie looked embarrassed.

"I've forgotten," he said. "I didn't make a note of all the moves."

A sarcastic voice broke in from the background.

"But *I* did," said John Christopher. "You were cheating—you made two moves at once."

After that, I am sorry to say, there was some disorder, and Drew had to threaten violence before peace was restored. I don't know who really won the squabble, and I don't think it matters. For I'm inclined to agree with what Purvis remarked as he picked up the robot checker-board and examined its wiring.

"You see," he said, "this little gadget is only a simple-minded cousin of Karl's—and look what it's done already. All these machines are beginning to make us look fools. Before long they'll start to disobey us without any Milquetoast interfering with their circuits. And then they'll start ordering us about—they're logical, after all, and won't stand any nonsense."

He sighed. "When that happens, there won't be a thing we can do about it. We'll just have to say to the dinosaurs: 'Move over a bit—here comes *homo sap*!' And the transistor shall inherit the earth."

There was no time for further pessimistic philosophy, for the door opened and Police Constable Wilkins stuck his head in. "Where's the owner of CGC 571?" he asked testily. "Oh—it's *you*, Mr. Purvis. Your rear light's out."

Harry looked at me sadly, then shrugged his shoulders in resignation. "You see," he said, "it's started already." And he went out into the night.

The Next Tenants

"The number of mad scientists who wish to conquer the world," said Harry Purvis, looking thoughtfully at his beer, "has been grossly exaggerated. In fact, I can remember encountering only a single one."

"Then there couldn't have been many others," commented Bill Temple, a little acidly. "It's not the sort of thing one would be likely to forget."

"I suppose not," replied Harry, with that air of irrefragible innocence which is so disconcerting to his critics. "And, as a matter of fact, this scientist wasn't really mad. There was no doubt, though, that he was out to conquer the world. Or if you want to be really precise—to let the world be conquered."

"And by whom?" asked George Whitley. "The Martians? Or the well-known little green men from Venus?"

"Neither of them. He was collaborating with someone a lot nearer home. You'll realize who I mean when I tell you he was a myrmecologist."

"A which-what?" asked George.

"Let him get on with the story," said Drew, from the other

side of the bar. "It's past ten, and if I can't get you all out by closing time *this* week, I'll lose my license."

"Thank you," said Harry with dignity, handing over his glass for a refill. "This all happened about two years ago, when I was on a mission in the Pacific. It was rather hush-hush, but in view of what's happened since there's no harm in talking about it. Three of us scientists were landed on a certain Pacific atoll not a thousand miles from Bikini, and given a week to set up some detection equipment. It was intended, of course, to keep an eye on our good friends and allies when they started playing with thermo-nuclear reactions—to pick some crumbs from the A.E.C.'s table, as it were. The Russians, naturally, were doing the same thing, and occasionally we ran into each other and then both sides would pretend that there was nobody here but us chickens.

"This atoll was supposed to be uninhabited, but this was a considerable error. It actually had a population of several hundred millions—"

"What!" gasped everybody.

"—several hundred millions," continued Purvis calmly, "of which number, one was human. I came across him when I went inland one day to have a look at the scenery."

"Inland?" asked George Whitley. "I thought you said it was an atoll. How can a ring of coral—"

"It was a very plump atoll," said Harry firmly. "Anyway, who's telling this story?" He waited defiantly for a moment until he had the right of way again.

"Here I was, then, walking up a charming little river-course underneath the coconut palms, when to my great surprise I came across a waterwheel—a very modern-looking one, driving a dynamo. If I'd been sensible, I suppose I'd have gone back and told my companions, but I couldn't resist the challenge and decided to do some reconnoitering on my own. I remembered that there were still supposed to be Japanese troops around who didn't know that the war was over, but that explanation seemed a bit unlikely.

"I followed the power-line up a hill, and there on the other side was a low, whitewashed building set in a large clearing. All over this clearing were tall, irregular mounds of earth, linked together with a network of wires. It was one of the most baffling sights I have ever seen, and I stood and stared for a good ten minutes, trying to decide what was going on. The longer I looked, the less sense it seemed to make.

"I was debating what to do when a tall, white-haired man came out of the building and walked over to one of the mounds. He was carrying some kind of apparatus and had a pair of earphones slung around his neck, so I guessed that he was using a Geiger counter. It was just about then that I realized what those tall mounds were. They were termitaries . . . the skyscrapers, in comparison to their makers, far taller than the Empire State Building, in which the so-called white ants live.

"I watched with great interest, but complete bafflement, while the elderly scientist inserted his apparatus into the base of the termitary, listened intently for a moment, and then walked back towards the building. By this time I was so curious that I decided to make my presence known. Whatever research was going on here obviously had nothing to do with international politics, so I was the only one who'd have anything to hide. You'll appreciate later just what a miscalculation *that* was.

"I yelled for attention and walked down the hill, waving my arms. The stranger halted and watched me approaching: he didn't look particularly surprised. As I came closer I saw that he had a straggling moustache that gave him a faintly Oriental appearance. He was about sixty years old, and carried himself very erect. Though he was wearing nothing but a pair of shorts, he looked so dignified that I felt rather ashamed of my noisy approach.

"'Good morning,' I said apologetically. 'I didn't know that there was anyone else on this island. I'm with an—er—scientific survey party over on the other side.'

"At this, the stranger's eyes lit up. 'Ah,' he said, in almost perfect English, 'a fellow scientist! I'm very pleased to meet you. Come into the house.'

"I followed gladly enough—I was pretty hot after my scramble—and I found that the building was simply one large lab. In a corner was a bed and a couple of chairs, together with a stove and one of those folding wash-basins that campers use. That seemed to sum up the living arrangements. But everything was very neat and tidy: my unknown friend seemed to be a recluse, but he believed in keeping up appearances.

"I introduced myself first, and as I'd hoped he promptly responded. He was one Professor Takato, a biologist from a leading Japanese university. He didn't look particularly Japanese, apart from the moustache I've mentioned. With his erect, dignified bearing he reminded me more of an old Kentucky colonel I once knew.

"After he'd given me some unfamiliar but refreshing wine, we sat and talked for a couple of hours. Like most scientists he seemed happy to meet someone who would appreciate his work. It was true that my interests lay in physics and chemistry rather than on the biological side, but I found Professor Takato's research quite fascinating.

"I don't suppose you know much about termites, so I'll remind you of the salient facts. They're among the most highly evolved of the social insects, and live in vast colonies throughout the tropics. They can't stand cold weather, nor, oddly enough, can they endure direct sunlight. When they have to get from one place to another, they construct little covered roadways. They seem to have some unknown and almost instantaneous means of communication, and though the individual termites are pretty helpless and dumb, a whole colony behaves like an intelligent animal. Some writers have drawn comparisons between a termitary and a human body, which is also composed of individual living cells making up an entity much higher than the basic units. The termites are often called 'white ants', but that's a completely incorrect name as they aren't ants at all but quite a different species of insect. Or should I say 'genus'? I'm pretty vague about this sort of thing. . . .

"Excuse this little lecture, but after I'd listened to Takato for a while I began to get quite enthusiastic about termites myself. Did you know, for example, that they not only cultivate gardens but also keep cows—insect cows, of course—and milk them? Yes, they're sophisticated little devils, even though they do it all by instinct.

"But I'd better tell you something about the Professor. Although he was alone at the moment, and had lived on the island for several years, he had a number of assistants who brought equipment from Japan and helped him in his work. His first great achievement was to do for the termites what von Frische had done with bees—he'd learned their language. It was much more complex than the system of communication that bees use, which as you probably know, is based on dancing. I understood that the network of wires linking the termitaries to the lab not only enabled Professor Takato to listen to the termites talking among each other, but also permitted him to speak to them. That's not really as fantastic as it sounds, if you use the word "speak" in its widest sense. We speak to a good many animals—not always with our voices, by any means. When you throw a stick for your dog and expect him to run and fetch it, that's a form of speech—sign language. The Professor, I gathered, had worked out some kind of code which the termites understood, though how efficient it was at communicating ideas I didn't know.

"I came back each day, when I could spare the time, and by the end of the week we were firm friends. It may surprise you that I was able to conceal these visits from my colleagues, but the island was quite large and we each did a lot of exploring. I felt somehow that Professor Takato was my private property, and did not wish to expose him to the curiosity of my companions. They were rather uncouth characters—graduates of some provincial university like Oxford or Cambridge.

"I'm glad to say that I was able to give the Professor a certain amount of assistance, fixing his radio and lining up some of his electronic gear. He used radioactive tracers a good deal, to follow individual termites around. He'd been tracking one with a Geiger counter when I first met him, in fact.

"Four or five days after we'd met, his counters started to go haywire, and the equipment we'd set up began to reel in its recordings. Takato guessed what had happened: he'd never asked me exactly what I was doing on the islands, but I think he knew. When I greeted him he switched on his counters and let me listen to the roar of radiation. There had been some radioactive fall-out—not enough to be dangerous, but sufficient to bring the background 'way up.

" 'I think,' he said softly, 'that you physicists are playing with your toys again. And very big ones, this time.'

" 'I'm afraid you're right,' I answered. We wouldn't be sure until the readings had been analyzed, but it looked as if Teller and his team had started the hydrogen reaction. 'Before long, we'll be able to make the first A-bombs look like damp squibs.'

" 'My family,' said Professor Takato, without any emotion, 'was at Nagasaki.'

"There wasn't a great deal I could say to that, and I was glad when he went on to add: 'Have you ever wondered who will take over when we are finished?'

" 'Your termites?' I said, half facetiously. He seemed to hesitate for a moment. Then he said quietly, 'Come with me; I have not shown you everything.'

"We walked over to a corner of the lab where some equipment lay concealed beneath dust-sheets, and the Professor uncovered a rather curious piece of apparatus. At first sight it looked like one of the manipulators used for the remote handling of dangerously radioactive materials. There were handgrips that conveyed movements through rods and levers, but everything seemed to focus on a small box a few inches on a side. 'What is it?' I asked.

" 'It's a micromanipulator. The French developed them for biological work. There aren't many around yet.'

"Then I remembered. These were devices with which, by the use of suitable reduction gearing, one could carry out the most incredibly delicate operations. You moved your finger an inch—and the tool you were controlling moved a thousandth of an inch. The French scientists who had developed this technique had built tiny forges on which they could construct minute scalpels and tweezers from fused glass. Working entirely through microscopes, they had been able to dissect individual cells. Removing an appendix from a termite (in the highly doubtful event of the insect possessing one) would be child's play with such an instrument.

" 'I am not very skilled at using the manipulator,' confessed Takato. 'One of my assistants does all the work with it. I have shown no one else this, but you have been very helpful. Come with me, please.'

"We went out into the open, and walked past the avenues of tall, cement-hard mounds. They were not all of the same architectural design, for there are many different kinds of termites—some, indeed, don't build mounds at all. I felt rather like a giant walking through Manhattan, for these were skyscrapers, each with its own teeming population.

"There was a small metal (not wooden—the termites would soon have fixed that!) hut beside one of the mounds, and as we entered it the glare of sunlight was banished. The Professor threw a switch, and a faint red glow enabled me to see various types of optical equipment.

" 'They hate light,' he said, 'so it's a great problem observing them. We solved it by using infra-red. This is an image-converter of the type that was used in the war for operations at night. You know about them?'

" 'Of course,' I said. 'Snipers had them fixed on their rifles so that they could go sharp-shooting in the dark. Very ingenious things—I'm glad you've found a civilized use for them.'

"It was a long time before Professor Takato found what he wanted. He seemed to be steering some kind of periscope arrangement, probing through the corridors of the termite city. Then he said: 'Quick—before they've gone!'

"I moved over and took his position. It was a second or so before my eye focused properly, and longer still before I understood the scale of the picture I was seeing. Then I saw six termites, greatly enlarged, moving rather rapidly across the field of vision. They were travelling in a group, like the huskies forming a dog-team. And that was a very good analogy, because they were towing a sledge. . . .

"I was so astonished that I never even noticed what kind of load they were moving. When they had vanished from sight, I turned to Professor Takato. My eyes had now grown accustomed to the faint red glow, and I could see him quite well.

" 'So that's the sort of tool you've been building with your micromanipulator!' I said. 'It's amazing—I'd never have believed it.'

" 'But that is nothing,' replied the Professor. 'Performing

fleas will pull a cart around. I haven't told you what is so important. We only made a few of those sledges. *The one you saw they constructed themselves*.'

"He let that sink in: it took some time. Then he continued quietly, but with a kind of controlled enthusiasm in his voice: 'Remember that the termites, as individuals, have virtually no intelligence. But the colony as a whole is a very high type of organism—and an immortal one, barring accidents. It froze in its present instinctive pattern millions of years before Man was born, and by itself it can never escape from its present sterile perfection. It has reached a dead-end—because it has no tools, no effective way of controlling nature. I have given it the lever, to increase its power, and now the sledge, to improve its efficiency. I have thought of the wheel, but it is best to let that wait for a later stage—it would not be very useful now. The results have exceeded my expectations. I started with this termitary alone—but now they all have the same tools. They have taught each other, and that proves they can cooperate. True, they have wars—but not when there is enough food for all, as there is here.

" 'But you cannot judge the termitary by human standards. What I hope to do is to jolt its rigid, frozen culture—to knock it out of the groove in which it has stuck for so many millions of years. I will give it more tools, more new techniques—and before I die, I hope to see it beginning to invent things for itself.'

" 'Why are you doing this?' I asked, for I knew there was more than mere scientific curiosity here.

" 'Because I do not believe that Man will survive, yet I hope to preserve some of the things he has discovered. If he is to be a dead-end, I think that another race should be given a helping hand. Do you know why I chose this island? It was so that my experiment should remain isolated. My supertermite, if it ever evolves, will have to remain here until it has reached a very high level of attainment. Until it can cross the Pacific, in fact. . . .

" 'There is another possibility. Man has no rival on this planet. I think it may do him good to have one. It may be his salvation.'

"I could think of nothing to say: this glimpse of the Professor's dreams was so overwhelming—and yet, in view of what I had just seen, so convincing. For I knew that Professor Takato was not mad. He was a visionary, and there was a sublime detachment about his outlook, but it was based on a secure foundation of scientific achievement.

"And it was not that he was hostile to mankind: he was sorry for it. He simply believed that humanity had shot its bolt, and wished to save something from the wreckage. I could not feel it in my heart to blame him.

"We must have been in that little hut for a long time, exploring possible futures. I remember suggesting that perhaps there might be some kind of mutual understanding, since two cultures so utterly dissimilar as Man and Termite need have no cause for conflict. But I couldn't really believe this, and if a contest comes, I'm not certain who will win. For what use would man's weapons be against an intelligent enemy who could lay waste all the wheat fields and all the rice crops in the world?

"When we came out into the open once more, it was almost dusk. It was then that the Professor made his final revelation.

" 'In a few weeks,' he said, 'I am going to take the biggest step of all.'

" 'And what is that?' I asked.

" 'Cannot you guess? I am going to give them fire.'

"Those words did something to my spine. I felt a chill that had nothing to do with the oncoming night. The glorious sunset that was taking place beyond the palms seemed symbolic—

and suddenly I realized that the symbolism was even deeper than I had thought.

"That sunset was one of the most beautiful I had ever seen, and it was partly of man's making. Up there in the stratosphere, the dust of an island that had died this day was encircling the earth. My race had taken a great step forward; but did it matter now?

" '*I am going to give them fire*.' Somehow, I never doubted that the Professor would succeed. And when he had done so, the forces that my own race had just unleashed would not save it. . . .

"The flying boat came to collect us the next day, and I did not see Takato again. He is still there, and I think he is the most important man in the world. While our politicians wrangle, he is making us obsolete.

"Do you think that someone ought to stop him? There may still be time. I've often thought about it, but I've never been able to think of a really convincing reason why I should interfere. Once or twice I nearly made up my mind, but then I'd pick up the newspaper and see the headlines.

"I think we should let them have the chance. I don't see how they could make a worse job of it than we've done."

Moving Spirit

We were discussing a sensational trial at the Old Bailey when Harry Purvis, whose talent for twisting the conversation to his own ends is really unbelievable, remarked casually: "I was once an expert witness in a rather interesting case."

"Only a *witness*?" said Drew, as he deftly filled two glasses of Bass at once.

"Yes—but it was a rather close thing. It was in the early part of the war, about the time we were expecting the invasion. That's why you never heard about it at the time."

"What makes you assume," said Charles Willis suspiciously, "that we never did hear of it?"

It was one of the few times I'd ever seen Harry caught trying to cover up his tracks. "Qui s'excuse s'accuse," I thought to myself, and waited to see what evading action he'd take.

"It was such a peculiar case," he replied with dignity, "that I'm sure you'd have reminded me of it if you ever saw the reports. My name was featured quite prominently. It all happened in an out-of-the-way part of Cornwall, and it concerned the best example of that rare species, the genuine mad scientist, that I've ever met."

Perhaps that wasn't really a fair description, Purvis amended hastily. Homer Ferguson was eccentric and had little foibles like keeping a pet boa constrictor to catch the mice, and never wearing shoes around the house. But he was so rich that no one noticed things like this.

Homer was also a competent scientist. Many years ago he had graduated from Edinburgh University, but having plenty of money he had never done a stroke of real work in his life. Instead, he pottered round the old vicarage he'd bought not far from Newquay and amused himself building gadgets. In the last forty years he'd invented television, ball-point pens, jet propulsion, and a few other trifles. However, as he had never bothered to take out any patents, other people had got the credit. This didn't worry him in the least as he was of a singularly generous disposition, except with money.

It seemed that, in some complicated way, Purvis was one of his few living relatives. Consequently when Harry received a telegram one day requesting his assistance at once, he knew better than to refuse. No one knew exactly how much money Homer had, or what he intended to do with it. Harry thought he had as good a chance as anyone, and he didn't intend to jeopardize it. At some inconvenience he made the journey down to Cornwall and turned up at the rectory.

He saw what was wrong as soon as he entered the grounds. Uncle Homer (he wasn't really an uncle, but he'd been called that as long as Harry could remember) had a shed beside the main building which he used for his experiments. That shed was now minus roof and windows, and a sickly odor hovered around it. There had obviously been an explosion, and Harry wondered, in a disinterested sort of way, if Uncle had been badly injured and wanted advice on drawing up a new will.

He ceased day-dreaming when the old man, looking the picture of health (apart from some sticking plaster on his face) opened the door for him.

"Good of you to come so quickly," he boomed. He seemed genuinely pleased to see Harry. Then his face clouded over. "Fact is, my boy, I'm in a bit of a jam and I want you to help. My case comes up before the local Bench tomorrow."

This was a considerable shock. Homer had been as law-abiding a citizen as any motorist in petrol-rationed Britain could be expected to be. And if it was the usual black-market business, Harry didn't see how he could be expected to help.

"Sorry to hear about this, Uncle. What's the trouble?"

"It's a long story. Come into the library and we'll talk it over."

Homer Ferguson's library occupied the entire west wing of the somewhat decrepit building. Harry believed that bats nested in the rafters, but had never been able to prove it. When Homer had cleared a table by the simple expedient of tilting all the books off on to the floor, he whistled three times, a voice-operated relay tripped somewhere, and a gloomy Cornish voice drifted out of a concealed loudspeaker.

"Yes, Mr. Ferguson?"

"Maida, send across a bottle of the new whiskey."

There was no reply except an audible sniff. But a moment later there came a creaking and clanking, and a couple of square feet of library shelving slid aside to reveal a conveyor belt.

"I can't get Maida to come into the library," complained Homer, lifting out a loaded tray. "She's afraid of Boanerges, though he's perfectly harmless."

Harry found it hard not to feel some sympathy for the invisible Maida. All six feet of Boanerges was draped over the case holding the "Encyclopaedia Britannica", and a bulge amidships indicated that he had dined recently.

"What do you think of the whiskey?" asked Homer when Harry had sampled some and started to gasp for breath.

"It's—well, I don't know what to say. It's—phew—rather strong. I never thought—"

"Oh, don't take any notice of the label on the bottle. *This* brand never saw Scotland. And that's what all the trouble's about. I made it right here on the premises."

"Uncle!"

"Yes, I know it's against the law, and all that sort of nonsense. But you can't get any good whiskey these days—it all goes for export. It seemed to me that I was being patriotic making my own, so that there was more left over for the dollar drive. But the Excise people don't see it that way."

"I think you'd better let me have the whole story," said Harry. He was gloomily sure that there was nothing he could do to get his uncle out of this scrape.

Homer had always been fond of the bottle, and wartime shortages had hit him badly. He was also, as has been hinted, disinclined to give away money, and for a long time he had resented the fact that he had to pay a tax of several hundred percent on a bottle of whiskey. When he couldn't get his own supply any more, he had decided it was time to act.

The district he was living in probably had a good deal to do with his decision. For some centuries, the Customs and Excise had waged a never-ending battle with the Cornish fisherfolk. It was rumored that the last incumbent of the old vicarage had possessed the finest cellar in the district next to that of the Bishop himself—and had never paid a penny in duty on it. So Uncle Homer merely felt he was carrying on an old and noble tradition.

There was little doubt, moreover, that the spirit of pure scientific enquiry also inspired him. He felt sure that this business about being aged in the wood for seven years was all rubbish, and was confident that he could do a better job with ultrasonics and ultra-violet rays.

The experiment went well for a few weeks. But late one evening there was one of those unfortunate accidents that will happen even in the best-conducted laboratories, and before

Uncle knew what had happened, he was draped over a beam, while the grounds of the vicarage were littered with pieces of copper tubing.

Even then it would not have mattered much had not the local Home Guard been practicing in the neighborhood. As soon as they heard the explosion, they immediately went into action, Sten guns at the ready. Had the invasion started? If so, they'd soon fix it.

They were a little disappointed to discover that it was only Uncle, but as they were used to his experiments they weren't in the least surprised at what had happened. Unfortunately for Uncle, the Lieutenant in charge of the squad happened to be the local exciseman, and the combined evidence of his nose and his eyes told him the story in a flash.

"So tomorrow," said Uncle Homer, looking rather like a small boy who had been caught stealing candy, "I have to go up before the Bench, charged with possessing an illegal still."

"I should have thought," replied Harry, "that was a matter for the Assizes, not the local magistrates."

"We do things our own way here," answered Homer, with more than a touch of pride. Harry was soon to discover how true this was.

They got little sleep that night, as Homer outlined his defence, overcame Harry's objections, and hastily assembled the apparatus he intended to produce in court.

"A Bench like this," he explained, "is always impressed by experts. If we dared, I'd like to say you were someone from the War Office, but they could check up on that. So we'll just tell them the truth—about your qualifications, that is."

"Thank you," said Harry. "And suppose my college finds out what I'm doing?"

"Well, you won't claim to be acting for anyone except yourself. The whole thing is a private venture."

"I'll say it is," said Harry.

The next morning they loaded their gear into Homer's ancient Austin, and drove into the village. The Bench was sitting in one of the classrooms of the local school, and Harry felt that time had rolled back a few years and he was about to have an unpleasant interview with his old headmaster.

"We're in luck," whispered Homer, as they were ushered into their cramped seats. "Major Fotheringham is in the Chair. He's a good friend of mine."

That would help a lot, Harry agreed. But there were two other justices on the Bench as well, and one friend in court would hardly be sufficient. Eloquence, not influence, was the only thing that could save the day.

The courtroom was crowded, and Harry found it surprising that so many people had managed to get away from work long enough to watch the case. Then he realized the local interest that it would have aroused, in view of the fact that—in normal times, at least—smuggling was a major industry in these parts. He was not sure whether that would mean a sympathetic audience. The natives might well regard Homer's form of private enterprise as unfair competition. On the other hand, they probably approved on general principles with anything that put the excisemen's noses out of joint.

The charge was read by the clerk of the court, and the somewhat damning evidence produced. Pieces of copper tubing were solemnly inspected by the justices, each of whom in turn looked severely at Uncle Homer. Harry began to see his hypothetical inheritance becoming even more doubtful.

When the case for the prosecution was completed, Major Fotheringham turned to Homer.

"This appears to be a serious matter, Mr. Ferguson. I hope you have a satisfactory explanation."

"I have, your Honor," replied the defendant in a tone that

practically reeked of injured innocence. It was amusing to see His Honor's look of relief, and the momentary frown, quickly replaced by calm confidence, that passed across the face of H. M. Customs and Excise.

"Do you wish to have a legal representative? I notice that you have not brought one with you."

"It won't be necessary. The whole case is founded on such a trivial misunderstanding that it can be cleared up without complications like that. I don't wish to incur the prosecution in unnecessary costs."

This frontal onslaught brought a murmur from the body of the court, and a flush to the cheeks of the Customs man. For the first time he began to look a little unsure of himself. If Ferguson thought the Crown would be paying costs, he must have a pretty good case. Of course, he might only be bluffing. . . .

Homer waited until the mild stir had died away before creating a considerably greater one.

"I have called a scientific expert to explain what happened at the Vicarage," he said. "And owing to the nature of the evidence, I must ask, for security reasons, that the rest of the proceedings be *in camera*."

"You want me to clear the court?" said the Chairman incredulously.

"I am afraid so, sir. My colleague, Doctor Purvis, feels that the fewer people concerned in this case, the better. When you have heard the evidence, I think you will agree with him. If I might say so, it is a great pity that it has already attracted so much publicity. I am afraid it may bring certain—ah—confidential matters to the wrong ears."

Homer glared at the customs officer, who fidgeted uncomfortably in his seat.

"Oh, very well," said Major Fotheringham. "This is all very irregular, but we live in irregular times. Mr. Clerk, clear the court."

After some grumbling and confusion, and an overruled protest from the prosecution, the order was carried out. Then, under the interested gaze of the dozen people left in the room, Harry Purvis uncovered the apparatus he had unloaded from the Baby Austin. After his qualifications had been presented to the court, he took the witness stand.

"I wish to explain, your Honor," he began, "that I have been engaged on explosives research, and that is why I happen to be acquainted with the defendant's work." The opening part of this statement was perfectly true. It was about the last thing said that day that was.

"You mean—bombs and so forth?"

"Precisely, but on a fundamental level. We are always looking for new and better types of explosives, as you can imagine. Moreover, we in government research and the academic world are continually on the lookout for good ideas from outside sources. And quite recently, Unc—er, Mr. Ferguson, wrote to us with a most interesting suggestion for a completely new type of explosive. The interesting thing about it was that it employed *non-explosive* materials such as sugar, starch and so on."

"Eh?" said the Chairman. "A non-explosive explosive? That's impossible."

Harry smiled sweetly.

"I know, sir—that is one's immediate reaction. But like most great ideas, this has the simplicity of genius. I am afraid, however, that I shall have to do a little explaining to make my point."

The Bench looked very attentive, and also a little alarmed. Harry surmised that it had probably encountered expert witnesses before. He walked over to a table that had been set up in the middle of the courtroom, and which was now covered with flasks, piping, and bottles of liquids.

"I hope, Mr. Purvis," said the Chairman nervously, "that you're not going to do anything dangerous."

"Of course not, sir. I merely wish to demonstrate some basic scientific principles. Once again, I wish to stress the importance of keeping this between these four walls." He paused solemnly and everyone looked duly impressed.

"Mr. Ferguson," he began, "is proposing to tap one of the fundamental forces of nature. It is a force on which every living thing depends—a force, gentlemen, which keeps *you* alive, even though you may never have heard of it."

He moved over to the table and took up his position beside the flasks and bottles.

"Have you ever stopped to consider," he said, "how the sap manages to reach the highest leaf of a tall tree? It takes a lot of force to pump water a hundred—sometimes over three hundred—feet from the ground. Where does that force come from? I'll show you, with this practical example.

"Here I have a strong container, divided into two parts by a porous membrane. On one side of the membrane is pure water—on the other, a concentrated solution of sugar and other chemicals which I do not propose to specify. Under these conditions, a pressure is set up, known as *osmotic* pressure. The pure water tries to pass through the membrane, as if to dilute the solution on the other side. I've now sealed the container, and you'll notice the pressure gauge here on the right—see how the pointer's going up. That's osmotic pressure for you. This same force acts through the cell walls in our bodies, causing fluid movement. It drives the sap up the trunk of trees, from the roots to the topmost branches. It's a universal force, and a powerful one. To Mr. Ferguson must go the credit of first attempting to harness it."

Harry paused impressively and looked round the court.

"Mr. Ferguson," he said, "was attempting to develop the Osmotic Bomb."

It took some time for this to sink in. Then Major Fotheringham leaned forward and said in a hushed voice: "Are we to presume that he had succeeded in manufacturing this bomb, and that it exploded in his workshop?"

"Precisely, your Honor. It is a pleasure—an unusual pleasure, I might say—to present a case to so perspicacious a court. Mr. Ferguson had succeeded, and he was preparing to report his method to us when, owing to an unfortunate oversight, a safety device attached to the bomb failed to operate. The results, you all know. I think you will need no further evidence of the power of this weapon—and you will realize its importance when I point out that the solutions it contains are all extremely common chemicals."

Major Fotheringham, looking a little puzzled, turned to the prosecution lawyer.

"Mr. Whiting," he said, "have you any questions to ask the witness?"

"I certainly have, your Honor. I've never heard such a ridiculous—"

"You will please confine yourself to questions of fact."

"Very good, your Honor. May I ask the witness how he accounts for the large quantity of alcohol vapor immediately after the explosion?"

"I rather doubt if the inspector's nose was capable of accurate quantitative analysis. But admittedly there was some alcohol vapor released. The solution used in the bomb contained about 25 percent. By employing dilute alcohol, the mobility of the inorganic ions is restricted and the osmotic pressure raised—a desirable effect, of course."

That should hold them for a while, thought Harry. He was right. It was a good couple of minutes before the second question. Then the prosecution's spokesman waved one of the pieces of copper tubing in the air.

"What function did these carry out?" he said, in as nasty a tone of voice as he could manage. Harry affected not to notice the sneer.

"Manometer tubing for the pressure gauges," he replied promptly.

The Bench, it was clear, was already far out of its depth. This was just where Harry wanted it to be. But the prosecution still had one card up its sleeve. There was a furtive whispering between the exciseman and his legal eagle. Harry looked nervously at Uncle Homer, who shrugged his shoulders with a "Don't ask *me*!" gesture.

"I have some additional evidence I wish to present to the Court," said the Customs lawyer briskly, as a bulky brown paper parcel was hoisted on to the table.

"Is this in order, your Honor?" protested Harry. "All evidence against my—ah—colleague should already have been presented."

"I withdraw my statement," the lawyer interjected swiftly. "Let us say that this is not evidence for *this* case, but material for later proceedings." He paused ominously to let that sink in. "Nevertheless, if Mr. Ferguson can give a satisfactory answer to our questions now, this whole business can be cleared up right away." It was obvious that the last thing the speaker expected—or hoped for—was such a satisfactory explanation.

He unwrapped the brown paper, and there were three bottles of a famous brand of whiskey.

"Uh-huh," said Uncle Homer. "I was wondering—"

"Mr. Ferguson," said the Chairman of the Bench. "There is no need for you to make any statement unless you wish."

Harry Purvis shot Major Fotheringham a grateful glance. He guessed what had happened. The prosecution had, when prowling through the ruins of Uncle's laboratory, acquired some bottles of his home-brew. Their action was probably illegal, since they would not have had a search-warrant—hence the reluctance in producing the evidence. The case had seemed sufficiently clear-cut without it.

It certainly appeared pretty clear-cut now. . . .

"These bottles," said the representative of the Crown, "do not contain the brand advertised on the label. They have obviously been used as convenient receptacles for the defendent's—shall we say—chemical solutions." He gave Harry Purvis an unsympathetic glance. "We have had these solutions analyzed, with most interesting results. Apart from an abnormally high alcohol concentration, the contents of these bottles are virtually indistinguishable from—"

He never had time to finish his unsolicited and certainly unwanted testimonial to Uncle Homer's skill. For at that moment, Harry Purvis became aware of an ominous whistling sound. At first he thought it was a falling bomb—but that seemed unlikely, as there had been no air raid warning. Then he realized that the whistling came from close at hand; from the courtroom table, in fact. . . .

"Take cover!" he yelled.

The Court went into recess with a speed never matched in the annals of British law. The three justices disappeared behind the dais; those in the body of the room burrowed into the floor or sheltered under desks. For a protracted, anguished moment nothing happened, and Harry wondered if he had given a false alarm. Then there was a dull, peculiarly muffled explosion, a great tinkling of glass—and a smell like a blitzed brewery. Slowly, the Court emerged from shelter.

The Osmotic Bomb had proved its power. More important still, it had destroyed the evidence for the prosecution.

The Bench was none too happy about dismissing the case; it felt, with good reason, that its dignity had been assailed. Moreover, each one of the justices would have to do some fast talking when he got home: the mist of alcohol had penetrated everything. Though the Clerk of the Court rushed round opening windows (none of which, oddly enough, had been broken) the fumes seemed reluctant to disperse. Harry Purvis, as he removed pieces of bottle-glass from his hair, wondered if there would be some intoxicated pupils in class tomorrow.

Major Fotheringham, however, was undoubtedly a real sport, and as they filed out of the devastated courtroom, Harry heard him say to his Uncle: "Look here, Ferguson—it'll be ages before we can get those Molotov Cocktails we've been promised by the War Office. What about making some of these bombs of yours for the Home Guard? If they don't knock out a tank, at least they'll make the crew drunk and incapable."

"I'll certainly think about it, Major," replied Uncle Homer, who still seemed a little dazed by the turn of events.

He recovered somewhat as they drove back to the Vicarage along the narrow, winding lane with their high walls of unmortared stone.

"I hope, Uncle," remarked Harry, when they had reached a relatively straight stretch and it seemed safe to talk to the driver, "that you don't intend to rebuild that still. They'll be watching you like hawks and you won't get away with it again."

"Very well," said Uncle, a little sulkily. "Confound these brakes! I had them fixed only just before the War!"

"Hey!" cried Harry, "Watch out!"

It was too late. They had come to a cross-roads at which a brand-new HALT sign had been erected. Uncle braked hard, but for a moment nothing happened. Then the wheels on the left seized up, while those on the right continued gaily spinning. The car did a hairpin bend, luckily without turning over, and ended in the ditch pointing in the direction from which it had come.

Harry looked reproachfully at his Uncle. He was about to frame a suitable reprimand when a motor-cycle came out of the side-turning and drew up to them.

It was not going to be their lucky day, after all. The village police-sergeant had been lurking in ambush, waiting to catch motorists at the new sign. He parked his machine by the roadside and leaned in through the window of the Austin.

"You all right, Mr. Ferguson?" he said. Then his nose wrinkled up, and he looked like Jove about to deliver a thunderbolt. "This won't do," he said. "I'll have to put you on a charge. Driving under the influence is a *very* serious business."

"But I've not touched a drop all day!" protested Uncle, waving an alcohol-sodden sleeve under the sergeant's twitching nose.

"Do you expect me to believe *that*?" snorted the irate policeman, pulling out his note-book. "I'm afraid you'll have to come to the station with me. Is your friend sober enough to drive?"

Harry Purvis didn't answer for a moment. He was too busy beating his head against the dash-board.

"Well," we asked Harry. "What did they do to your Uncle?"

"Oh, he got fined five pounds and had his license endorsed for drunken driving. Major Fotheringham wasn't in the Chair, unfortunately, when the case came up, but the other two justices were still on the Bench. I guess they felt that even if he was innocent this time, there was a limit to everything."

"And did you ever get any of his money?"

"No fear! He was very grateful, of course, and he's told me that I'm mentioned in his will. But when I saw him last, what do you think he was doing? He was searching for the Elixir of Life."

Harry sighed at the overwhelming injustice of things.

"Sometimes," he said gloomily, "I'm afraid he's found it. The doctors say he's the healthiest seventy-year-old they've ever seen. So all I got out of the whole affair was some interesting memories and a hangover."

"A hangover?" asked Charlie Willis.

"Yes," replied Harry, a faraway look in his eye. "You see, the excise men hadn't seized *all* the evidence. We had to—ah—destroy the rest. It took us the best part of a week. We invented all sorts of things during that time—but we never discovered what they were."

The Man Who Ploughed the Sea

The adventures of Harry Purvis have a kind of mad logic that makes them convincing by their very improbability. As his complicated but neatly dove-tailed stories emerge, one becomes lost in a sort of baffled wonder. Surely, you say to yourself, no-one would have the nerve to make *that* up—such absurdities only occur in real life, not in fiction. And so criticism is disarmed, or at any rate discomfitted, until Drew shouts, "Time, gentlemen, *pleeze*!" and throws us all out into the cold hard world.

Consider, for example, the unlikely chain of events which involved Harry in the following adventure. If he'd wanted to invent the whole thing, surely he could have managed it a lot more simply. There was not the slightest need, from the artistic point of view, to have started at Boston to make an appointment off the coast of Florida. . . .

Harry seems to have spent a good deal of time in the United States, and to have quite as many friends there as he has in England. Sometimes he brings them to the "White Hart," and sometimes they leave again under their own power. Often, however, they succumb to the illusion that beer which is tepid is also innocuous. (I am being unjust to Drew: his beer is *not* tepid. And if you insist, he will give you, for no extra charge, a piece of ice every bit as large as a postage-stamp.)

This particular saga of Harry's began, as I have indicated, at Boston, Mass. He was staying as a house-guest of a successful New England lawyer when one morning his host said, in the casual way Americans have: "Let's go down to my place in Florida. I want to get some sun."

"Fine," said Harry, who'd never been to Florida. Thirty minutes later, to his considerable surprise, he found himself moving south in a red Jaguar saloon at a formidable speed.

The drive in itself was an epic worthy of a complete story. From Boston to Miami is a little matter of 1,568 miles—a figure which, according to Harry, is now engraved on his heart. They covered the distance in 30 hours, frequently to the sound of ever-receding police sirens as frustrated squad-cars dwindled astern. From time to time considerations of tactics involved them in evasive manoeuvres and they had to shoot off into secondary roads. The Jaguar's radio tuned in to all the police frequencies, so they always had plenty of warning if an interception was being arranged. Once or twice they just managed to reach a state line in time, and Harry couldn't help wondering what his host's clients would have thought had they known the strength of the psychological urge which was obviously getting him away from them. He also wondered if he was going to see anything of Florida at all, or whether they would continue at this velocity down US 1 until they shot into the ocean at Key West.

They finally came to a halt sixty miles south of Miami, down on the Keys—that long, thin line of island hooked on to the lower end of Florida. The Jaguar angled suddenly off the road and weaved a way through a rough track cut in the mangroves. The road ended in a wide clearing at the edge of the sea, complete with dock, 35 foot cabin cruiser, swimming pool, and modern ranch-type house. It was a quite a nice little hideaway, and Harry estimated that it must have cost the best part of a hundred thousand dollars.

He didn't see much of the place until the next day, as he collapsed straight into bed. After what seemed far too short a time, he was awakened by a sound like a boiler factory in action. He showered and dressed in slow motion, and was reasonably back to normal by the time he had left his room. There seemed to be no one in the house, so he went outside to explore.

By this time he had learned not to be surprised at anything, so he barely raised his eyebrows when he found his host working down at the dock, straightening out the rudder on a tiny and obviously home-made submarine. The little craft was about twenty feet long, had a conning tower with large observation windows, and bore the name "Pompano" stencilled on her prow.

After some reflection, Harry decided that there was nothing really very unusual about all this. About five million visitors come to Florida every year, most of them determined to get on or into the sea. His host happened to be one of those fortunate enough to indulge in his hobby in a big way.

Harry looked at the "Pompano" for some time, and then a disturbing thought struck him. "George," he said, "do you expect me to go down in *that* thing?"

"Why, sure," answered George, giving a final bash at the rudder. "What are you worried about? I've taken her out lots of times—she's safe as houses. We won't be going deeper than twenty feet."

"There are circumstances," retorted Harry, "when I should find a mere six feet of water more than adequate. And didn't I mention my claustrophobia? It always comes on badly at this time of year."

"Nonsense!" said George. "You'll forget all about that when

we're out on the reef." He stood back and surveyed his handiwork, then said with a sigh of satisfaction, "Looks O.K. now. Let's have some breakfast."

During the next thirty minutes, Harry learned a good deal about the "Pompano." George had designed and built her himself, and her powerful little diesel could drive her at five knots when she was fully submerged. Both crew and engine breathed through a snorkle tube, so there was no need to bother about electric motors and an independent air supply. The length of the snorkle limited dives to twenty-five feet, but in these shallow waters this was no great handicap.

"I've put a lot of novel ideas into her," said George enthusiastically. "Those windows, for instance—look at their size. They'll give you a perfect view, yet they're quite safe. I use the old Aqualung principle to keep the air-pressure in the 'Pompano' exactly the same as the water-pressure outside, so there's no strain on the hull or the ports."

"And what happens," asked Harry, "if you get stuck on the bottom?"

"I open the door and get out, of course. There are a couple of spare Aqualungs in the cabin, as well as a life-raft with a waterproof radio, so that we can always yell for help if we get in trouble. Don't worry—I've thought of everything."

"Famous last words," muttered Harry. But he decided that after the ride down from Boston he undoubtedly had a charmed life: the sea was probably a safer place than US 1 with George at the wheel.

He made himself thoroughly familiar with the escape arrangements before they set out, and was fairly happy when he saw how well designed and constructed the little craft appeared to be. The fact that a lawyer had produced such a neat piece of marine engineering in his spare time was not in the least unusual. Harry had long ago discovered that a considerable number of Americans put quite as much effort into their hobbies as into their professions.

They chugged out of the little harbour, keeping to the marked channel until they were well clear of the coast. The sea was calm and as the shore receded the water became steadily more and more transparent. They were leaving behind the fog of pulverized coral which clouded the coastal waters, where the waves were incessantly tearing at the land. After thirty minutes they had come to the reef, visible below them as a kind of patchwork quilt above which multicolored fish pirouetted to and fro. George closed the hatches, opened the valve of the buoyancy tanks, and said gaily, "Here we go!"

The wrinkled silk veil lifted, crept past the window, distorting all vision for a moment—and then they were through, no longer aliens looking into the world of waters, but denizens of that world themselves. They were floating above a valley carpeted with white sand, and surrounded by low hills of coral. The valley itself was barren but the hills around it were alive with things that grew, things that crawled and things that swam. Fish as dazzling as neon signs wandered lazily among the animals that looked like trees. It seemed not only a breathtakingly lovely but also a peaceful world. There was no haste, no sign of the struggle for existence. Harry knew very well that this was an illusion, but during all the time they were submerged he never saw one fish attack another. He mentioned this to George, who commented: "Yes, that's a funny thing about fish. They seem to have definite feeding times. You can see barracuda swimming around and if the dinner gong hasn't gone the other fish won't take any notice of them."

A ray, looking like some fantastic black butterfly, flapped its way across the sand, balancing itself with its long, whiplike tail. The sensitive feelers of a crayfish waved cautiously from a crack in the coral; the exploring gestures reminded Harry of a soldier testing for snipers with his hat on a stick. There was so much life, of so many kinds, crammed in this single spot that it would take years of study to recognize it all.

The "Pompano" cruised very slowly along the valley, while George gave a running commentary.

"I used to do this sort of thing with the Aqualung," he said, "but then I decided how nice it would be to sit in comfort and have an engine to push me around. Then I could stay out all day, take a meal along, use my cameras and not give a damn if a shark was sneaking up on me. There goes a tang—did you ever see such a brilliant blue in your life? Besides, I could show my friends around down here while still being able to talk to them. That's one big handicap with ordinary diving gear—you're deaf and dumb and have to talk in signs. Look at those angelfish—one day I'm going to fix up a net to catch some of them. See the way they vanish when they're edge-on! Another reason why I built the 'Pompano' was so that I could look for wrecks. There are hundreds in this area—it's an absolute graveyard. The 'Santa Margarita' is only about fifty miles from here, in Biscayne Bay. She went down in 1595 with seven million dollars of bullion aboard. And there's a little matter of sixty-five million off Long Cay, where fourteen galleons sank in 1715. The trouble is, of course, that most of these wrecks have been smashed up and overgrown with coral, so it wouldn't do you a lot of good even if you did locate them. But it's fun to try."

By this time Harry had begun to appreciate his friend's psychology. He could think of few better ways of escaping from a New England law practice. George was a repressed romantic—and not such a repressed one, either, now that he came to think of it.

They cruised along happily for a couple of hours, keeping in water that was never more than forty feet deep. Once they grounded on a dazzling stretch of broken coral, and took time off for liverwurst sandwiches and glasses of beer. "I drank some ginger beer down here once," said George. "When I came up the gas inside me expanded and it was a very odd sort of feeling. Must try it with champagne some day."

Harry was just wondering what to do with the empties when the "Pompano" seemed to go into eclipse as a dark shadow drifted overhead. Looking up through the observation window, he saw that a ship was moving slowly past twenty feet above their heads. There was no danger of a collision, as they had pulled down their snort for just this reason and were subsisting for the moment on their capital as far as air was concerned. Harry had never seen a ship from underneath and began to add another novel experience to the many he had acquired today.

He was quite proud of the fact that, despite his ignorance of matters nautical, he was just as quick as George at spotting what was wrong with the vessel sailing overhead. Instead of the normal shaft and screw, this ship had a long tunnel running the length of its keel. As it passed above them, the "Pompano" was rocked by the sudden rush of water.

"I'll be damned!" said George, grabbing the controls. "That looks like some kind of jet propulsion system. It's about time somebody tried one out. Let's have a look."

He pushed up the periscope, and discovered that the ship slowly cruising past them was the "Valency," of New Orleans. "That's a funny name," he said. "What does it mean?"

"I would say," answered Harry, "that it means the owner is a chemist—except for the fact that no chemist would ever make enough money to buy a ship like that."

"I'm going to follow her," decided George. "She's only making five knots, and I'd like to see how that dingus works."

He elevated the snort, got the diesel running, and started in pursuit. After a brief chase, the "Pompano" drew within fifty feet of the "Valency," and Harry felt rather like a submarine commander about to launch a torpedo. They couldn't miss from this distance.

In fact, they nearly made a direct hit. For the "Valency" suddenly slowed to a halt, and before George realized what had happened, he was alongside her. "No signals!" he complained, without much logic. A minute later, it was clear that the manoeuvre was no accident. A lasso dropped neatly over the "Pompano's" snorkle and they were efficiently gaffed. There was nothing to do but emerge, rather sheepishly, and make the best of it.

Fortunately, their captors were reasonable men and could recognize the truth when they heard it. Fifteen minutes after coming aboard the "Valency," George and Harry were sitting on the bridge while a uniformed steward brought them highballs and they listened attentively to the theories of Dr. Gilbert Romano.

They were still both a little overawed at being in Dr. Romano's presence: it was rather like meeting a live Rockefeller or a reigning du Pont. The Doctor was a phenomenon virtually unknown in Europe and unusual even in the United States—the big scientist who had become a bigger business man. He was now in his late seventies and had just been retired—after a considerable tussle—from the chairmanship of the vast chemical engineering firm he had founded.

It is rather amusing, Harry told us, to notice the subtle social distinctions which differences in wealth can produce even in the most democratic country. By Harry's standards, George was a very rich man: his income was around a hundred thousand dollars a year. But Dr. Romano was in another price range altogether, and had to be treated accordingly with a kind of friendly respect which had nothing to do with obsequiousness. On his side, the Doctor was perfectly free and easy; there was nothing about him that gave any impression of wealth, if one ignored such trivia as hundred-and-fifty-foot ocean-going yachts.

The fact that George was on first-name terms with most of the Doctor's business acquaintances helped to break the ice and to establish the purity of their motives. Harry spent a boring half hour while business deals ranging over half the United States were discussed in terms of what Bill So-and-so did in Pittsburgh, who Joe Somebody Else ran into at the Bankers' Club in Houston, how Clyde Thingummy happened to be playing golf at Augusta while Ike was there. It was glimpse of a mysterious world where immense power was wielded by men who all seemed to have gone to the same colleges, or who at any rate belonged to the same clubs. Harry soon became aware of the fact that George was not merely paying court to Dr. Romano because that was the polite thing to do. George was too shrewd a lawyer to miss this chance of building up some good-will, and appeared to have forgotten all about the original purpose of their expedition.

Harry had to wait for a suitable gap in the conversation before he could raise the subject which really interested him. When it dawned on Dr. Romano that he was talking to another scientist, he promptly abandoned finance and George was the one who was left out in the cold.

The thing that puzzled Harry was why a distinguished chemist should be interested in marine propulsion. Being a man of direct action, he challenged the Doctor on this point. For a moment the scientist appeared a little embarrassed and Harry was about to apologize for his inquisitiveness—a feat that would have required real effort on his part. But before he could do this, Dr. Romano had excused himself and disappeared into the bridge.

He came back five minutes later with a rather satisfied expression, and continued as if nothing had happened.

"A very natural question, Mr. Purvis," he chuckled. "I'd have asked it myself. But do you really expect me to tell you?"

"Er—it was just a vague sort of hope," confessed Harry.

"Then I'm going to surprise you—surprise you twice, in fact. I'm going to answer you, and I'm going to show you that I'm *not* passionately interested in marine propulsion. Those bulges on the bottom of my ship which you were inspecting with such great interest do contain the screws, but they also contain a good deal else as well.

"Let me give you," continued Dr. Romano, now obviously warming up to his subject, "a few elementary statistics about the ocean. We can see a lot of it from here—quite a few square miles. Did you know that every cubic mile of sea-water contains a hundred and fifty *million* tons of minerals."

"Frankly, no," said George. "It's an impressive thought."

"It's impressed me for a long time," said the Doctor. "Here we go grubbing about in the earth for our metals and chemicals, while every element that exists can be found in sea water. The ocean, in fact, is a kind of universal mine which can never be exhausted. We may plunder the land, but we'll never empty the sea.

"Men have already started to mine the sea, you know. Dow Chemicals have been taking out bromine for years: every cubic mile contains about three hundred thousand tons. More recently, we've started to do something about the five million tons of magnesium per cubic mile. But that sort of thing is merely a beginning.

"The great practical problem is that most of the elements present in sea-water are in such low concentrations. The first seven elements make up about 99 percent of the total, and it's the remaining one percent that contains all the useful metals except magnesium.

"All my life I've wondered how we could do something about this, and the answer came during the war. I don't know if you're familiar with the techniques used in the atomic energy field to remove minute quantities of isotopes from solutions: some of those methods are still pretty much under wraps."

"Are you talking about ion-exchange resins?" hazarded Harry.

"Well—something similar. My firm developed several of these techniques on A.E.C. contracts, and I realized at once that they would have wider applications. I put some of my bright young men to work and they have made what we call a "molecular sieve". That's a mighty descriptive expression: in its way, the thing *is* a sieve, and we can set it to select anything we like. It depends on very advanced wave-mechanical theories for its operation, but what it actually does is absurdly simple. We can choose any component of sea-water we like, and get the sieve to take it out. With several units, working in series, we can take out one element after another. The efficiency's quite high, and the power consumption negligible."

"I know!" yelped George. "You're extracting gold from sea-water!"

"Huh!" snorted Dr. Romano in tolerant disgust. "I've got better things to do with my time. Too much damn gold around, anyhow. I'm after the commercially useful metals—the ones our civilisation is going to be desperately short of in another couple of generations. And as a matter of fact, even with my sieve it wouldn't be worth going after gold. There are only about fifty pounds of the stuff in every cubic mile."

"What about uranium?" asked Harry. "Or is that scarcer still?"

"I rather wish you hadn't asked that question," replied Dr. Romano with a cheerfulness that belied the remark. "But since you can look it up in any library, there's no harm in telling you that uranium's two hundred times *more* common than gold. About seven tons in every cubic mile—a figure which is, shall we say, distinctly interesting. So why bother about gold?"

"Why indeed?" echoed George.

"To continue," said Dr. Romano, duly continuing, "even with the molecular sieve, we've still got the problem of processing enormous volumes of sea-water. There are a number of ways one could tackle this: you could build giant pumping stations, for example. But I've always been keen on killing two birds with one stone, and the other day I did a little calculation that gave the most surprising result. I found that every time the 'Queen Mary' crosses the Atlantic, her screws chew up about a tenth of a cubic mile of water. Fifteen million tons of minerals, in other words. Or to take the case you indiscreetly mentioned—almost a ton of uranium on every Atlantic crossing. Quite a thought, isn't it?

"So it seemed to me that all we need do to create a very useful mobile extraction plant was to put the screws of any vessel inside a tube which would compel the slip-stream to pass through one of my sieves. Of course, there's a certain loss of propulsive power, but our experimental unit works very well. We can't go quite as fast as we did, but the further we cruise the more money we make from our mining operations. Don't you think the shipping companies will find that very attractive? But of course that's merely incidental. I look forward to the building of floating extraction plants that will cruise round and round in the ocean until they've filled their hoppers with anything you care to name. When that day comes, we'll be able to stop tearing up the land and all our material shortages will be over. Everything goes back to the sea in the long run anyway, and once we've unlocked that treasure-chest, we'll be all set for eternity."

For a moment there was silence on deck, save for the faint clink of ice in the tumblers, while Dr. Romano's guests contemplated this dazzling prospect. Then Harry was struck by a sudden thought.

"This is quite one of the most important inventions I've ever heard of," he said. "That's why I find it rather odd that you should have confided in us so fully. After all, we're perfect strangers, and for all you know might be spying on you."

The old scientist chortled gaily.

"Don't worry about *that*, my boy," he reassured Harry. "I've already been on to Washington and had my friends check up on you."

Harry blinked for a minute, then realized how it had been done. He remembered Dr. Romano's brief disappearance, and could picture what had happened. There would have been a radio call to Washington, some senator would have got on to the Embassy, the Ministry of Supply representative would have done his bit—and in five minutes the Doctor would have got the answer he wanted. Yes, Americans were very efficient—those who could afford to be.

It was about this time that Harry became aware of the fact that they were no longer alone. A much larger and more impressive yacht than the "Valency" was heading towards them, and in a few minutes he was able to read the name "Sea Spray". Such a name, he thought, was more appropriate to billowing sails than throbbing diesels, but there was no doubt that the "Spray" was a very pretty creature indeed. He could understand the looks of undisguised covetousness that both George and Dr. Romano now plainly bore.

The sea was so calm that the two yachts were able to come alongside each other, and as soon as they had made contact a sunburned, energetic man in the late forties vaulted over on to the deck of the "Valency". He strode up to Dr. Romano, shook his hand vigorously, said, "Well, you old rascal, what are you up to?" and then looked enquiringly at the rest of the company. The Doctor carried out the introductions: it seemed that they had been boarded by Professor Scott McKenzie, who'd been sailing *his* yacht down from Key Largo.

"Oh no!" cried Harry to himself. "This is *too* much! One millionaire scientist per day is all I can stand."

But there was no getting away from it. True, McKenzie was very seldom seen in the academic cloisters, but he was a genuine Professor none the less, holding the chair of geophysics at some Texas college. Ninety percent of his time, however, he spent working for the big oil companies and running a consulting firm of his own. It rather looked as if he had made his torsion balances and seismographs pay quite well for themselves. In fact, though he was a much younger man than Dr. Romano, he had even more money owing to being in a more rapidly expanding industry. Harry gathered that the peculiar tax laws of the Sovereign State of Texas also had something to do with it. . . .

It seemed an unlikely coincidence that these two scientific tycoons should have met by chance, and Harry waited to see what skullduggery was afoot. For a while the conversation was confined to generalities, but it was obvious that Professor McKenzie was extremely inquisitive about the Doctor's other two guests. Not long after they had been introduced, he made some excuse to hop back to his own ship and Harry moaned inwardly. If the Embassy got two separate enquiries about him in the space of half an hour, they'd wonder what he'd been up to. It might even make the F.B.I. suspicious, and then how would he get those promised twenty-four pairs of nylons out of the country?

Harry found it quite fascinating to study the relation between the two scientists. They were like a couple of fighting cocks circling for position. Romano treated the younger man with a downright rudeness which, Harry suspected, concealed a grudging admiration. It was clear that Dr. Romano was an almost fanatical conservationist, and regarded the activities of McKenzie and his employers with the greatest disapproval. "You're a gang of robbers," he said once. "You're seeing how quickly you can loot this planet of its resources, and you don't give a damn about the next generation."

"And what," answered McKenzie, not very originally, "has the next generation ever done for us?"

The sparring continued for the best part of an hour, and much of what went on was completely over Harry's head. He wondered why he and George were being allowed to sit in on all this, and after a while he began to appreciate Dr. Romano's technique. He was an opportunist of genius: he was glad to keep them round, now that they had turned up, just to worry Professor McKenzie and to make him wonder what other deals were afoot.

He let the molecular sieve leak out bit by bit, as if it wasn't *really* important and he was only mentioning it in passing. Professor McKenzie, however, latched on to it at once, and the more evasive Romano became, the more insistent was his adversary. It was obvious that he was being deliberately coy, and that though Professor McKenzie knew this perfectly well, he couldn't help playing the older scientist's game.

Dr. Romano had been discussing the device in a peculiarly oblique fashion, as if it were a future project rather than an existing fact. He outlined its staggering possibilities, and explained how it would make all existing forms of mining obsolete, besides removing forever the danger of world metal shortages.

"If it's so good," exclaimed McKenzie presently, "why haven't you made the thing?"

"What do you think I'm doing out here in the Gulf Stream?" retorted the Doctor. "Take a look at this."

He opened a locker beneath the sonar set, and pulled out a small metal bar which he tossed to McKenzie. It looked like lead, and was obviously extremely heavy. The Professor hefted it in his hand and said at once: "Uranium. Do you mean to say. . . ."

"Yes—every gram. And there's plenty more where that came from." He turned to Harry's friend and said: "George—what about taking the Professor down in your submarine to have a look at the works? He won't see much, but it'll show him we're in business."

McKenzie was still so thoughtful that he took a little thing like a private submarine in his stride. He returned to the surface fifteen minutes later, having seen just enough to whet his appetite.

"The first thing I want to know," he said to Romano, "is why you're showing this to *me*! It's about the biggest thing that ever happened—why isn't your own firm handling it?"

Romano gave a little snort of disgust.

"You know I've had a row with the Board," he said. "Anyway, that lot of old dead-beats couldn't handle anything as big as this. I hate to admit it, but you Texas pirates are the boys for the job."

"This is a private venture of yours?"

"Yes: the company knows nothing about it, and I've sunk half a million of my own money into it. It's been a kind of hobby of mine. I felt someone had to undo the damage that was going on, the rape of the continents by people like—"

"All right—we've heard that before. Yet you propose giving it to us?"

"Who said anything about giving?"

There was a pregnant silence. Then McKenzie said cautiously; "Of course, there's no need to tell you that we'll be interested—very interested. If you'll let us have the figures on efficiency, extraction rates, and all the other relevant statistics—no need to tell us the actual technical details if you don't want to—then we'll be able to talk business. I can't really speak for my associates but I'm sure that they can raise enough cover to make any deal—"

"Scott," said Romano—and his voice now held a note of tiredness that for the first time reflected his age—"I'm not interested in doing a deal with your partners. I haven't time to haggle with the boys in the front room and their lawyers and their lawyers' lawyers. Fifty years I've been doing that sort of thing, and believe me, I'm tired. This is *my* development. It was done with *my* money, and all the equipment is in *my* ship. I want to do a personal deal, direct with you. You can handle it from then on."

McKenzie blinked.

"I couldn't swing anything as big as this," he protested. "Sure, I appreciate the offer, but if this does what you say, it's worth billions. And I'm just a poor but honest millionaire."

"Money I'm no longer interested in. What would I do with it at my time of life? No, Scott, there's just one thing I want now—and I want it right away, this minute. Give me the 'Sea Spray', and you can have my process."

"You're crazy! Why, even with inflation, you could build the 'Spray' for inside a million. And your process must be worth—"

"I'm not arguing, Scott. What you say is true, but I'm an old man in a hurry, and it would take me a year to get a ship like yours built. I've wanted her ever since you showed her to me back at Miami. My proposal is that you take over the 'Valency', with all her lab equipment and records. It will only take an hour to swap our personal effects—we've a lawyer here who can make it all legal. And then I'm heading out into the Caribbean, down through the islands, and across the Pacific."

"You've got it all worked out?" said McKenzie in awed wonder.

"Yes. You can take it or leave it."

"I never heard such a crazy deal in my life," said McKenzie, somewhat petulantly. "Of course I'll take it. I know a stubborn old mule when I see one."

The next hour was one of frantic activity. Sweating crew-members rushed back and forth with suitcases and bundles, while Dr. Romano sat happily in the midst of the turmoil he had created, a blissful smile upon his wrinkled old face. George and Professor McKenzie went into a legal huddle, and emerged with a document which Dr. Romano signed with hardly a glance.

Unexpected things began to emerge from the "Sea Spray", such as a beautiful mutation mink and a beautiful non-mutation blonde.

"Hello, Sylvia," said Dr. Romano politely. "I'm afraid you'll find the quarters here a little more cramped. The Professor never mentioned you were aboard. Never mind—we won't mention it either. Not actually in the contract, but a gentleman's agreement, shall we say? It would be such a pity to upset Mrs. McKenzie."

"I don't know *what* you mean!" pouted Sylvia. "Someone has to do all the Professor's typing."

"And you do it damn badly, my dear," said McKenzie, assisting her over the rail with true Southern gallantry. Harry couldn't help admiring his composure in such an embarrassing situation—he was by no means sure that he would have managed as well. But he wished he had the opportunity to find out.

At last the chaos subsided, the stream of boxes and bundles subsided to a trickle. Dr. Romano shook hands with everybody, thanked George and Harry for their assistance, strode to the bridge of the "Sea Spray", and ten minutes later, was halfway to the horizon.

Harry was wondering if it wasn't about time for them to

take their departure as well—they had never got round to explaining to Professor McKenzie what they were doing here in the first place—when the radio-telephone started calling. Dr. Romano was on the line.

"Forgotten his tooth-brush, I suppose," said George. It was not quite as trivial as that. Fortunately, the loudspeaker was switched on. Eavesdropping was practically forced upon them and required none of the effort that makes it so embarrassing to a gentleman.

"Look here, Scott," said Dr. Romano, "I think I owe you some sort of explanation."

"If you've gypped me, I'll have you for every cent—"

"Oh, it's not like that. But I did rather pressurize you, though everything I said was perfectly true. Don't get too annoyed with me—you've got a bargain. It'll be a long time, though, before it makes you any money, and you'll have to sink a few millions of your own into it first. You see, the efficiency has to be increased by about three orders of magnitude before it will be a commercial proposition: that bar of uranium cost me a couple of thousand dollars. Now don't blow your top—it *can* be done—I'm certain of that. Dr. Kendall is the man to get: he did all the basic work—hire him away from my people however much it costs you. You're a stubborn cuss and I know you'll finish the job now it's on your hands. That's why I wanted you to have it. Poetic justice, too—you'll be able to repay some of the damage you've done to the land. Too bad it'll make you a billionaire, but that can't be helped.

"Wait a minute—don't cut in on me. I'd have finished the job myself if I had the time, but it'll take at least three more years. And the doctors say I've only got six months: I wasn't kidding when I said I was in a hurry. I'm glad I clinched the deal without having to tell you that, but believe me I'd have used it as a weapon if I had to. Just one thing more—when you do get the process working, name it after me, will you? That's all—it's no use calling me back. I won't answer—and I know you can't catch me."

Professor McKenzie didn't turn a hair.

"I thought it was something like that," he said to no one in particular. Then he sat down, produced an elaborate pocket slide-rule, and became oblivious to the world. He scarcely looked up when George and Harry, feeling very much outclassed, made their polite departure and silently snorkled away.

"Like so many things that happen these days," concluded Harry Purvis, "I still don't know the final outcome of this meeting. I rather imagine that Professor McKenzie has run into some snags, or we'd have heard rumors about the process by now. But I've not the slightest doubt that sooner or later it'll be perfected, so get ready to sell your mining shares. . . .

"As for Dr. Romano, he wasn't kidding, though his doctors were a little out in their estimates. He lasted a full year, and I guess the 'Sea Spray' helped a lot. They buried him in mid-Pacific, and it's just occurred to me that the old boy would have appreciated that. I told you what a fanatical conservationist he was, and it's a piquant thought that even now some of his atoms may be going through his own molecular sieve. . . .

"I notice some incredulous looks, but it's a fact. If you took a tumbler of water, poured it into the ocean, mixed well, then filled the glass from the sea, there'd still be some scores of molecules of water from the original sample in the tumbler. So—" he gave a gruesome little chuckle—"it's only a matter of time before not only Dr. Romano, but all of us, make some contribution to the sieve. And with that thought, gentlemen, I bid you all a very pleasant good-night."

The Reluctant Orchid

Though few people in the "White Hart" will concede that any of Harry Purvis' stories are actually *true*, everyone agrees that some are much more probable than others. And on any scale of probability, the affair of the Reluctant Orchid must rate very low indeed.

I don't remember what ingenious gambit Harry used to launch this narrative: maybe some orchid fancier brought his latest monstrosity into the bar, and that set him off. No matter. I do remember the story, and after all that's what counts.

The adventure did not, this time, concern any of Harry's numerous relatives, and he avoided explaining just how he managed to know so many of the sordid details. The hero—if you can call him that—of this hothouse epic was an inoffensive little clerk named Hercules Keating. And if you think *that* is the most unlikely part of the story, just stick round a while.

Hercules is not the sort of name you can carry off lightly at the best of times, and when you are four foot nine and look as if you'd have to take a physical culture course before you can even become a 97-pound weakling, it is a positive embarrassment. Perhaps it helped to explain why Hercules had very little social life, and all his real friends grew in pots in a humid conservatory at the bottom of his garden. His needs were simple and he spent very little money on himself; consequently his collection of orchids and cacti was really rather remarkable. Indeed, he had a wide reputation among the fraternity of cactophiles, and often received from remote corners of the globe, parcels smelling of mould and tropical jungles.

Hercules had only one living relative, and it would have been hard to find a greater contrast than Aunt Henrietta. She was a massive six footer, usually wore a rather loud line in Harris tweeds, drove a Jaguar with reckless skill, and chain-smoked cigars. Her parents had set their hearts on a boy, and had never been able to decide whether or not their wish had been granted. Henrietta earned a living, and quite a good one, breeding dogs of various shapes and sizes. She was seldom without a couple of her latest models, and they were not the type of portable canine which ladies like to carry in their handbags. The Keating Kennels specialized in Great Danes, Alsatians, and Saint Bernards. . . .

Henrietta, rightly despising men as the weaker sex, had never married. However, for some reason she took an avuncular (yes, that is definitely the right word) interest in Hercules, and called to see him almost every weekend. It was a curious kind of relationship: probably Henrietta found that Hercules bolstered up her feelings of superiority. If he was a good example of the male sex, then they were certainly a pretty sorry lot. Yet, if this was Henrietta's motivation, she was unconscious of it and seemed genuinely fond of her nephew. She was patronizing, but never unkind.

As might be expected, her attentions did not exactly help Hercules' own well-developed inferiority complex. At first he had tolerated his aunt; then he came to dread her regular visits, her booming voice and her bone-crushing handshake; and at last he grew to hate her. Eventually, indeed, his hate was the dominant emotion in his life, exceeding even his love for his orchids. But he was careful not to show it, realizing that if Aunt Henrietta discovered how he felt about her, she would probably break him in two and throw the pieces to her wolf pack.

There was no way, then, in which Hercules could express his pent-up feelings. He had to be polite to Aunt Henrietta even when he felt like murder. And he often did feel like murder, though he knew that there was nothing he would ever do about it. Until one day . . .

According to the dealer, the orchid came from "somewhere in the Amazon region"—a rather vague postal address. When Hercules first saw it, it was not a very pre-possessing sight, even to anyone who loved orchids as much as he did. A shapeless root, about the size of a man's fist—that was all. It was redolent of decay, and there was the faintest hint of a rank, carrion smell. Hercules was not even sure that it was viable, and told the dealer as much. Perhaps that enabled him to purchase it for a trifling sum, and he carried it home without much enthusiasm.

It showed no signs of life for the first month, but that did not worry Hercules. Then, one day, a tiny green shoot appeared and started to creep up to the light. After that, progress was rapid. Soon there was a thick, fleshy stem as big as a man's forearm, and colored a positively virulent green. Near the top of the stem a series of curious bulges circled the plant: otherwise it was completely featureless. Hercules was now quite excited: he was sure that some entirely new species had swum into his ken.

The rate of growth was now really fantastic: soon the plant was taller than Hercules, not that that was saying a great deal. Moreover, the bulges seemed to be developing, and it looked as if at any moment the orchid would burst into bloom. Hercules waited anxiously, knowing how short-lived some flowers can be, and spent as much time as he possibly could in the hot-house. Despite all his watchfulness, the transformation occurred one night while he was asleep.

In the morning, the orchid was fringed by a series of eight dangling tendrils, almost reaching to the ground. They must have developed inside the plant and emerged with—for the vegetable world—explosive speed. Hercules stared at the phenomenon in amazement, and went very thoughtfully to work.

That evening, as he watered the plant and checked its soil, he noticed a still more peculiar fact. The tendrils were thickening, and they were not completely motionless. They had a slight but unmistakable tendency to vibrate, as if possessing a life of their own. Even Hercules, for all his interest and enthusiasm, found this more than a little disturbing.

A few days later, there was no doubt about it at all. When he approached the orchid, the tendrils swayed towards him in an unpleasantly suggestive fashion. The impression of hunger was so strong that Hercules began to feel very uncomfortable indeed, and something started to nag at the back of his mind. It was quite a while before he could recall what it was: then he said to himself, "Of course! How stupid of me!" and went along to the local library. Here he spent a most interesting half-hour rereading a little piece by one H. G. Wells entitled, "The Flowering of the Strange Orchid."

"My goodness!" thought Hercules, when he had finished the tale. As yet there had been no stupifying odor which might overpower the plant's intended victim, but otherwise the characteristics were all too similar. Hercules went home in a very unsettled mood indeed.

He opened the conservatory door and stood looking along the avenue of greenery towards his prize specimen. He judged the length of the tendrils—already he found himself calling them tentacles—with great care and walked to within what appeared a safe distance. The plant certainly had an impression of alertness and menace far more appropriate to the animal than the vegetable kingdom. Hercules remembered the unfortunate history of Doctor Frankenstein, and was not amused.

But, really, this was ridiculous! Such things didn't happen in real life. Well, there was one way to put matters to the test . . .

Hercules went into the house and came back a few minutes later with a broomstick, to the end of which he had attached a piece of raw meat. Feeling a considerable fool, he advanced towards the orchid as a lion-tamer might approach one of his charges at meal-time.

For a moment, nothing happened. Then two of the tendrils developed an agitated twitch. They began to sway back and forth, as if the plant was making up its mind. Abruptly, they whipped out with such speed that they practically vanished from view. They wrapped themselves round the meat, and Hercules felt a powerful tug at the end of his broomstick. Then the meat was gone: the orchid was clutching it, if one may mix metaphors slightly, to its bosom.

"Jumping Jehosophat!" yelled Hercules. It was very seldom indeed that he used such strong language.

The orchid showed no further signs of life for twenty-four hours. It was waiting for the meat to become high, and it was also developing its digestive system. By the next day, a network of what looked like short roots had covered the still visible chunk of meat. By nightfall, the meat was gone.

The plant had tasted blood.

Hercules' emotions as he watched over his prize were curiously mixed. There were times when it almost gave him nightmares, and he foresaw a whole range of horrid possibilities. The orchid was now extremely strong, and if he got within its clutches he would be done for. But, of course, there was not the slightest danger of that. He had arranged a system of pipes so that it could be watered from a safe distance, and its less orthodox food he simply tossed within range of its tentacles. It was now eating a pound of raw meat a day, and he had an uncomfortable feeling that it could cope with much larger quantities if given the opportunity.

Hercules' natural qualms were, on the whole, outweighed by his feeling of triumph that such a botanical marvel had fallen into his hands. Whenever he chose, he could become the most famous orchid-grower in the world. It was typical of his somewhat restricted view-point that it never occurred to him that other people besides orchid-fanciers might be interested in his pet.

The creature was now about six feet tall, and apparently still growing—though much more slowly than it had been. All the other plants had been moved from its end of the conservatory, not so much because Hercules feared that it might be cannibalistic as to enable him to tend them without danger. He had stretched a rope across the central aisle so that there was no risk of his accidentally walking within range of those eight dangling arms.

It was obvious that the orchid had a highly developed nervous system, and something very nearly approaching intelligence. It knew when it was going to be fed, and exhibited unmistakable signs of pleasure. Most fantastic of all—though Hercules was still not sure about this—it seemed capable of producing sounds. There were times, just before a meal, when he fancied he could hear an incredibly high-pitched whistle, skirting the edge of audibility. A new-born bat might have had such a voice: he wondered what purpose it served. Did the orchid somehow lure its prey into its clutches by sound? If so, he did not think the technique would work on him.

While Hercules was making these interesting discoveries, he continued to be fussed over by Aunt Henrietta and assaulted by her hounds, which were never as house-trained as she claimed them to be. She would usually roar up the street on a Sunday afternoon with one dog in the seat beside her and another occupying most of the baggage compartment. Then she would bound up the steps two at a time, nearly deafen Hercules with her greeting, half paralyze him with her handshake, and blow cigar smoke in his face. There had been a time when he was terrified that she would kiss him, but he had long since realized that such effeminate behaviour was foreign to her nature.

Aunt Henrietta looked upon Hercules' orchids with some scorn. Spending one's spare time in a hothouse was, she considered, a very effete recreation. When *she* wanted to let off steam, she went big-game hunting in Kenya. This did nothing to endear her to Hercules, who hated blood sports. But despite his mounting dislike for his over-powering aunt, every Sunday afternoon he dutifully prepared tea for her and they had a tête-à-tête together which, on the surface at least, seemed perfectly friendly. Henrietta never guessed that as he poured the tea Hercules often wished it was poisoned: she was, far down beneath her extensive fortifications, a fundamentally good-hearted person and the knowledge would have upset her deeply.

Hercules did not mention his vegetable octopus to Aunt Henrietta. He had occasionally shown her his most interesting specimens, but this was something he was keeping to himself. Perhaps, even before he had fully formulated his diabolical plan, his subconscious was already preparing the ground . . .

It was late one Sunday evening, when the roar of the Jaguar had died away into the night and Hercules was restoring his shattered nerves in the conservatory, that the idea first came fully-fledged into his mind. He was staring at the orchid, noting how the tendrils were now as thick around as a man's thumb, when a most pleasing fantasy suddenly flashed before his eyes. He pictured Aunt Henrietta struggling helplessly in the grip of the monster, unable to escape from its carnivorous clutches. Why, it would be the perfect crime. The distraught nephew would arrive on the scene too late to be of assistance, and when the police answered his frantic call they would see at a glance that the whole affair was a deplorable accident. True, there would be an inquest, but the coroner's censure would be toned down in view of Hercules' obvious grief . . .

The more he thought of the idea, the more he liked it. He could see no flaws, as long as the orchid co-operated. That, clearly, would be the greatest problem. He would have to plan a course of training for the creature. It already looked sufficiently diabolical; he must give it a disposition to suit its appearance.

Considering that he had no prior experience in such matters, and that there were no authorities he could consult, Hercules proceeded along very sound and businesslike lines. He would use a fishing rod to dangle pieces of meat just outside the orchid's range, until the creature lashed its tentacles in a frenzy. At such times its high-pitched squeak was clearly audible, and Hercules wondered how it managed to produce the sound. He also wondered what its organs of perception were, but this was yet another mystery that could not be solved without close examination. Perhaps Aunt Henrietta, if all went well, would have a brief opportunity of discovering these interesting facts—though she would probably be too busy to report them for the benefit of posterity.

There was no doubt that the beast was quite powerful enough to deal with its intended victim. It had once wrenched a broomstick out of Hercules' grip, and although that in itself proved very little, the sickening "crack" of the wood a moment later brought a smile of satisfaction to its trainer's thin lips. He began to be much more pleasant and attentive to his aunt. In every respect, indeed, he was the model nephew.

When Hercules considered that his picador tactics had brought the orchid into the right frame of mind, he wondered if he should test it with live bait. This was a problem that worried him for some weeks, during which time he would look speculatively at every dog or cat he passed in the street, but he finally abandoned the idea, for a rather peculiar reason. He was simply too kind-hearted to put it into practice. Aunt Henrietta would have to be the first victim.

He starved the orchid for two weeks before he put his plan into action. This was as long as he dared risk—he did not wish to weaken the beast—merely to whet its appetite that the outcome of the encounter might be more certain. And so, when he had carried the tea-cups back into the kitchen and was sitting upwind of Aunt Henrietta's cigar, he said casually: "I've got something I'd like to show you, auntie. I've been keeping it as a surprise. It'll tickle you to death."

That, he thought, was not a completely accurate description, but it gave the general idea.

Auntie took the cigar out of her mouth and looked at Hercules with frank surprise.

"Well!" she boomed. "Wonders will never cease! What *have* you been up to, you rascal?" She slapped him playfully on the back and shot all the air out of his lungs.

"You'll never believe it," gritted Hercules, when he had recovered his breath. "It's in the observatory."

"Eh?" said Auntie, obviously puzzled.

"Yes—come along and have a look. It's going to create a real sensation."

Auntie gave a snort that might have indicated disbelief, but followed Hercules without further question. The two Alsatians now busily chewing up the carpet looked at her anxiously and half rose to their feet, but she waved them away.

"All right, boys," she ordered gruffly. "I'll be back in a minute." Hercules thought this unlikely.

It was a dark evening, and the lights in the conservatory were off. As they entered, Auntie snorted, "Gad, Hercules—the place smells like a slaughter-house. Haven't met such a stink since I shot that elephant in Bulawayo and we couldn't find it for a week."

"Sorry, auntie," apologized Hercules, propelling her forward through the gloom. "It's a new fertilizer I'm using. It produces the most stunning results. Go on—another couple of yards. I want this to be a *real* surprise."

"I hope this isn't a joke," said Auntie suspiciously, as she stomped forward.

"I can promise you it's no joke," replied Hercules, standing with his hand on the light switch. He could just see the looming bulk of the orchid: Auntie was now within ten feet of it. He waited until she was well inside the danger zone, and threw the switch.

There was a frozen moment while the scene was transfixed with light. Then Aunt Henrietta ground to a halt and stood, arms akimbo, in front of the giant orchid. For a moment Hercules was afraid she would retreat before the plant could get into action: then he saw that she was calmly scrutinizing it, unable to make up her mind what the devil it was.

It was a full five seconds before the orchid moved. Then the dangling tentacles flashed into action—but not in the way that Hercules had expected. The plant clutched them tightly, protectively, *around itself*—and at the same time it gave a high-pitched scream of pure terror. In a moment of sickening disillusionment, Hercules realized the awful truth.

His orchid was an utter coward. It might be able to cope with the wild life of the Amazon jungle, but coming suddenly upon Aunt Henrietta had completely broken its nerve.

As for its proposed victim, she stood watching the creature with an astonishment which swiftly changed to another emotion. She spun around on her heels and pointed an accusing finger at her nephew.

"Hercules!" she roared. "The poor thing's scared to death. *Have you been bullying it?*"

Hercules could only stand with his head hanging low in shame and frustration.

"N-no, auntie," he quavered. "I guess it's naturally nervous."

"Well, I'm used to animals. You should have called me before. You must treat them firmly—but gently. Kindness always works, as long as you show them you're the master. There, there, did-dums—don't be frightened of auntie—she won't hurt you . . ."

It was, thought Hercules in his blank despair, a revolting sight. With surprising gentleness, Aunt Henrietta fussed over the beast, patting and stroking it until the tentacles relaxed and the shrill, whistling scream died away. After a few minutes of this pandering, it appeared to get over its fright. Hercules finally fled with a muffled sob when one of the tentacles crept forward and began to stroke Henrietta's gnarled fingers . . .

From that day, he was a broken man. What was worse, he could never escape from the consequences of his intended crime. Henrietta had acquired a new pet, and was liable to call not only at weekends but two or three times in between as well. It was obvious that she did not trust Hercules to treat the orchid properly, and still suspected him of bullying it. She would bring tasty tidbits that even her dogs had rejected, but which the orchid accepted with delight. The smell, which had so far been confined to the conservatory, began to creep into the house . . .

And there, concluded Harry Purvis, as he brought this improbable narrative to a close, the matter rests—to the satisfaction of two, at any rate, of the parties concerned. The orchid is happy, and Aunt Henrietta has something (query, someone?)

else to dominate. From time to time the creature has a nervous breakdown when a mouse gets loose in the conservatory, and she rushes to console it.

As for Hercules, there is no chance that he will ever give any more trouble to either of them. He seems to have sunk into a kind of vegetable sloth: indeed, said Harry thoughtfully, every day he becomes more and more like an orchid himself.

The harmless variety, of course. . . .

Cold War

One of the things that makes Harry Purvis' tales so infernally convincing is their detailed verisimilitude. Consider, for instance, this example. I've checked the places and information as thoroughly as I can—I had to, in order to write up this account—and everything fits into place. How do you explain that unless—but judge for yourself . . .

"I've often noticed," Harry began, "how tantalizing little snippets of information appear in the Press and then, sometimes years later, one comes across their sequels. I've just had a beautiful example. In the spring of 1954—I've looked up the date—it was April 19—an iceberg was reported off the coast of Florida. I remember spotting this news item and thinking it highly peculiar. The Gulf Stream, you know, is born in the Straits of Florida, and I didn't see *how* an iceberg could get that far south before it melted. But I forgot about the whole business almost immediately, thinking it was just another of those tall stories which the papers like to print when there isn't any real news.

"And then, about a week ago, I met a friend who'd been a Commander in the U.S. Navy, and he told me the whole astonishing tale. It's such a remarkable story that I think it ought to be better known, though I'm sure that a lot of people simply won't believe it.

"Any of you who are familiar with domestic American affairs may know that Florida's claim to be the Sunshine State is strongly disputed by some of the other forty-seven members of the Union. I don't suppose New York or Maine or Connecticut are very serious contenders, but the State of California regards the Florida claim as an almost personal affront, and is always doing its best to refute it. The Floridians hit back by pointing to the famous Los Angeles smogs, then the Californians say, with careful anxiety, "Isn't it about time you had another hurricane?' and the Floridians reply 'You can count on us when you want any earthquake relief.' So it goes on, and this is where my friend Commander Dawson came into the picture.

"The Commander had been in submarines, but was now retired. He'd been working as technical advisor on a film about the exploits of the submarine service when he was approached one day with a very peculiar proposition. I won't say that the California Chamber of Commerce was behind it, as that might be libel. You can make your own guesses . . .

"Anyway, the idea was a typical Hollywood conception. So I thought at first, until I remembered that dear old Lord Dunsany had used a similar theme in one of his short stories. Maybe the Californian sponsor was a Jorkens fan, just as I am.

"The scheme was delightful in its boldness and simplicity. Commander Dawson was offered a substantial sum of money to pilot an artificial iceberg to Florida, with a bonus if he could contrive to strand it on Miami Beach at the height of the season.

"I need hardly say that the Commander accepted with alacrity: he came from Kansas himself, so could view the whole thing dispassionately as a purely commercial proposition. He got together some of his old crew, swore them to secrecy, and after much waiting in Washington corridors managed to obtain temporary loan of an obsolete submarine. Then he went to a big air-conditioning company, convinced them of his credit and his sanity, and got the icemaking plant installed in a big blister on the sub's deck.

"It would take an impossible amount of power to make a solid iceberg, even a small one, so a compromise was necessary. There would be an outer coating of ice a couple of feet thick, but Frigid Freda, as she was christened, was to be hollow. She would look quite impressive from outside, but would be a typical Hollywood stage set when one got behind the scenes. However, nobody would see her inner secrets except the Commander and his men. She would be set adrift when the prevailing winds and currents were in the right direction, and would last long enough to cause the calculated alarm and despondency.

"Of course, there were endless practical problems to be solved. It would take several days of steady freezing to create Freda, and she must be launched as near her objective as possible. That meant that the submarine—which we'll call the *Marlin*—would have to use a base not too far from Miami.

"The Florida Keys were considered but at once rejected. There was no privacy down there any more; the fishermen now outnumbered the mosquitoes and a submarine would be spotted almost instantly. Even if the *Marlin* pretended she was merely smuggling, she wouldn't be able to get away with it. So that plan was out.

"There was another problem that the Commander had to consider. The coastal waters round Florida are extremely shallow, and though Freda's draught would only be a couple of feet, everybody knew that an honest-to-goodness iceberg was nearly all below the waterline. It wouldn't be very realistic to have an impressive-looking berg sailing through two feet of water. That would give the show away at once.

"I don't know exactly how the Commander overcame these technical problems, but I gather that he carried out several tests in the Atlantic, far from any shipping routes. The iceberg reported in the news was one of his early productions. Incidentally, neither Freda nor her brethren would have been a danger to shipping—being hollow, they would have broken up on impact.

Finally, all the preparations were complete. The *Marlin* lay out in the Atlantic, some distance north of Miami, with her ice-manufacturing equipment going full blast. It was a beautiful clear night, with a crescent moon sinking in the west. The *Marlin* had no navigation lights, but Commander Dawson was keeping a very strict watch for other ships. On a night like this, he'd be able to avoid them without being spotted himself.

"Freda was still in an embryonic stage. I gather that the technique used was to inflate a large plastic bag with super-cooled air, and spray water over it until a crust of ice formed. The bag could be removed when the ice was thick enough to stand up under its own weight. Ice is not a very good structural material, but there was no need for Freda to be very big. Even a small iceberg would be as disconcerting to the Florida Chamber of Commerce as a small baby to an unmarried lady.

"Commander Dawson was in the conning tower, watching his crew working with their sprays of ice-cold water and jets of freezing air. They were now quite skilled at this unusual occupation, and delighted in little artistic touches. However, the Commander had had to put a stop to attempts to reproduce Marilyn Monroe in ice—though he filed the idea for future reference.

"Just after midnight he was startled by a flash of light in the northern sky, and turned in time to see a red glow die away on the horizon.

" 'There's a plane down skipper!' shouted one of the lookouts. 'I just saw it crash!' Without hesitation, the Commander shouted down to the engine room and set course to the north. He'd got an accurate fix on the glow, and judged that it couldn't be more than a few miles away. The presence of Freda, covering most of the stern of his vessel, would not affect his speed appreciably, and in any case there was no way of getting rid of her quickly. He stopped the freezers to give more power to the main diesels, and shot ahead at full speed.

"About thirty minutes later the lookout, using powerful night-glasses, spotted something lying in the water. 'It's still afloat,' he said. 'Some kind of airplane all right—but I can't see any sign of life. And I think the wings have come off.'

"He had scarcely finished speaking when there was an urgent report from another watcher.

" 'Look, skipper—thirty degrees to starboard! What's that?'

"Commander Dawson swung around and whipped up his glasses. He saw, just visible above the water, a small oval object spinning rapidly on its axis.

" 'Uh-huh,' he said, 'I'm afraid we've got company. That's a radar scanner—there's another sub here.' Then he brightened considerably. 'Maybe we can keep out of this after all,' he remarked to his second in command. We'll watch to see that they start rescue operations, then sneak away.'

" 'We may have to submerge and abandon Freda. Remember they'll have spotted us by now on their radar. Better slacken speed and behave more like a real iceberg.'

"Dawson nodded and gave the order. This was getting complicated, and anything might happen in the next few minutes. The other sub would have observed the *Marlin* merely as a blip on its radar screen, but as soon as it upped periscope its commander would start investigating. Then the fat would be in the fire . . .

"Dawson analyzed the tactical situation. The best move, he decided, was to employ his unusual camouflage to the full. He gave the order to swing the *Marlin* around so that her stern pointed towards the still submerged stranger. When the other sub surfaced, her commander would be most surprised to see an iceberg, but Dawson hoped he would be too busy with rescue operations to bother about Freda.

"He pointed his glasses towards the crashed plane—and then had his second shock. It was a very peculiar type of aircraft indeed—and there was something wrong—

" 'Of course!' said Dawson to his Number One. 'We should have thought of this—that thing isn't an airplane at all. It's a missile from the range over at Cocoa—look, you can see the floatation bags. They must have inflated on impact, and that sub was waiting out here to take it back.'

"He'd remembered that there was a big missile launching range over on the east coast of Florida, at a place with the unlikely name of Cocoa on the still more improbable Banana River. Well, at least there was nobody in danger, and if the *Marlin* sat tight there was a sporting chance that they'd be none the worse for this diversion.

"Their engines were just turning over, so that they had enough control to keep hiding behind their camouflage. Freda was quite large enough to conceal their conning tower, and from a distance, even in better light than this, the *Marlin* would be totally invisible. There was one horrid possibility, though. The other sub might start shelling them on general principles, as a menace to navigation. No: it would just report them by radio to the coast-guards, which would be a nuisance but would not interfere with their plans.

" 'Here she comes!' said Number One. 'What class is she?'

"They both stared through their glasses as the submarine,

water pouring from its sides, emerged from the faintly phosphorescent ocean. The moon had now almost set, and it was difficult to make out any details. The radar scanner, Dawson was glad to see, had stopped its rotation and was pointing at the crashed missile. There was something odd about the design of that conning tower, though . . .

"Then Dawson swallowed hard, lifted the mike to his mouth, and whispered to his crew in the bowels of the *Marlin*: 'Does anyone down there speak Russian. . . .?'

"There was a long silence, but presently the engineer officer climbed up into the conning tower.

" 'I know a bit, skipper,' he said. 'My grandparents came from the Ukraine. What's the trouble?'

" 'Take a look at this,' said Dawson grimly. 'There's an interesting piece of poaching going on here. I think we ought to stop it . . .' "

Harry Purvis has a most annoying habit of breaking off just when a story reaches its climax, and ordering another beer—or, more usually, getting someone else to buy him one. I've watched him do this so often that now I can tell just when the climax is coming by the level in his glass. We had to wait, with what patience we could, while he refueled.

"When you think about it," he said thoughtfully, "it was jolly hard luck on the commander of that Russian submarine. I imagine they shot him when he got back to Vladivostock, or wherever he came from. For what court of inquiry would have believed his story? If he was fool enough to tell the truth, he'd have said, 'We were just off the Florida coast when an iceberg shouted at us in Russian, "Excuse me—I think that's *our* property!" ' Since there would be a couple of MVD men aboard the ship, the poor guy would have had to make up *some* kind of story, but whatever he said wouldn't be very convincing . . .

"As Dawson had calculated, the Russian sub simply ran for it as soon as it knew it had been spotted. And remembering that he was an officer on the reserve, and that his duty to his country was more important than his contractual obligations to any single state, the commander of the *Marlin* really had no choice in his subsequent actions. He picked up the missile, defrosted Freda, and set course for Cocoa—first sending a radio message that caused a great flurry in the Navy Department and started destroyers racing out into the Atlantic. Perhaps Inquisitive Ivan never got back to Valdivostock after all. . . .

"The subsequent explanations were a little embarrassing, but I gather that the rescued missile was so important that no one asked too many questions about the *Marlin*'s private war. The attack on Miami Beach had to be called off, however, at least until the next season. It's satisfactory to relate that even the sponsors of the project, though they had sunk a lot of money into it, weren't too disappointed. They each have a certificate signed by the Chief of Naval Operations, thanking them for valuable but unspecified services to their country. These cause such envy and mystification to all their Los Angeles friends that they wouldn't part with them for anything . . .

"Yet I don't want you to think that nothing more will ever come of the whole project; you ought to know American publicity men better than that. Freda may be in suspended animation, but one day she'll be revived. All the plans are ready, down to such little details as the accidental presence of a Hollywood film unit on Miami Beach when Freda comes sailing in from the Atlantic.

"So this is one of those stories I can't round off to a nice, neat ending. The preliminary skirmishes have taken place, but the main engagement is still to come. And this is the thing I often wonder about—*what will Florida do to the Californians when it discovers what's going on?* Any suggestions, anybody?"

What Goes Up

One of the reasons why I am never too specific about the exact location of the "White Hart" is frankly, because we want to keep it to ourselves. This is not merely a dog-in-the-manger attitude: we have to do it in pure self-protection. As soon as it gets around that scientists, editors and science-fiction writers are forgathering at some locality, the weirdest collection of visitors is likely to turn up. Peculiar people with new theories of the universe, characters who have been "cleared" by Dianetics (God knows what they were like before), intense ladies who are liable to go all clairvoyant after the fourth gin—these are the less exotic specimens. Worst of all, however, are the Flying Sorcerers: no cure short of mayhem has yet been discovered for them.

It was a black day when one of the leading exponents of the Flying Saucer religion discovered our hideout and fell upon us with shrill cries of delight. Here, he obviously told himself, was fertile ground for his missionary activities. People who were already interested in spaceflight, and even wrote books and stories about its imminent achievement, would be a pushover. He opened his little black bag and produced the latest pile of sauceriana.

It was quite a collection. There were some interesting photographs of flying saucers made by an amateur astronomer who lives right beside Greenwich Observatory, and whose busy camera has recorded such a remarkable variety of spaceships, in all shapes and sizes, that one wonders what the professionals next door are doing for their salaries. Then there was a long statement from a gentleman in Texas who had just had a casual chat with the occupants of a saucer making a wayside halt on route to Venus. Language, it seemed, had presented no difficulties: it had taken about ten minutes of arm-waving to get from "Me—Man. This—Earth" to highly esoteric information about the use of the fourth dimension in space-travel.

The masterpiece, however, was an excited letter from a character in South Dakota who had actually been offered a lift in a flying saucer, and had been taken for a spin round the Moon. He explained at some length how the saucer travelled by hauling itself along magnetic lines of force, rather like a spider going up its thread.

It was at this point that Harry Purvis rebelled. He had been listening with a professional pride to tales which even he would never have dared to spin, for he was an expert at detecting the yield-point of his audience's credulity. At the mention of lines of magnetic force, however, his scientific training overcame his frank admiration of these latter-day Munchausens, and he gave a snort of disgust.

"That's a lot of nonsense," he said. "I can prove it to you—magnetism's my speciality."

"Last week," said Drew sweetly, as he filled two glasses of ale at once, "you said that crystal structure was your speciality."

Harry gave him a superior smile.

"I'm a *general* specialist," he said loftily. "To get back to where I was before that interruption, the point I want to make is that there's no such thing as a line of magnetic force. It's a mathematical fiction—exactly on a par with lines of longitude or latitude. Now if anyone said they'd invented a machine that worked by pulling itself along parallels of latitude, everybody would know that they were talking drivel. But because few people know much about magnetism, and it sounds rather mysterious, crackpots like this guy in South Dakota can get away with the tripe we've just been hearing."

There's one charming characteristic about the "White Hart"—we may fight among each other, but we show an impressive solidarity in times of crisis. Everyone felt that something had to be done about our unwelcome visitor: for one thing, he was interfering with the serious business of drinking. Fanaticism of any kind casts a gloom over the most festive assembly, and several of the regulars had shown signs of leaving despite the fact that it was still two hours to closing time.

So when Harry Purvis followed up his attack by concocting the most outrageous story that even he had ever presented in the "White Hart", no one interrupted him or tried to expose the weak points in his narrative. We knew that Harry was acting for us all—he was fighting fire with fire, as it were. And we knew that he wasn't expecting us to believe him (if indeed he ever did) so we just sat back and enjoyed ourselves.

"If you want to know how to propel spaceships," began Harry, "and mark you, I'm not saying anything one way or the other about the existence of flying saucers—then you must forget magnetism. You must go straight to gravity—that's the basic force of the universe, after all. But it's going to be a tricky force to handle, and if you don't believe me just listen to what happened only last year to a scientist down in Australia. I shouldn't really tell you this, I suppose, because I'm not sure of its security classification, but if there's any trouble I'll swear that I never said a word.

"The Aussies, as you may know, have always been pretty hot on scientific research, and they had one team working on fast reactors—those house-broken atomic bombs which are so much more compact than the old uranium piles. The head of the group was a bright but rather impetuous young nuclear physicist I'll call Dr. Cavor. That, of course, wasn't his real name, but it's a very appropriate one. You'll all recollect, I'm sure, the scientist Cavor in Wells' FIRST MEN IN THE MOON, and the wonderful gravity-screening material Cavorite he discovered?

"I'm afraid dear old Wells didn't go into the question of Cavorite very thoroughly. As he put it, it was opaque to gravity just as a sheet of metal is opaque to light. Anything placed above a horizontal sheet of cavorite, therefore, became weightless and floated up into space.

"Well, it isn't as simple as that. Weight represents energy—an enormous amount of it—which can't just be destroyed without any fuss. You'd have to put a terrific amount of work into even a small object in order to make it weightless. Antigravity screens of the cavorite type, therefore, are quite impossible—they're in the same class as perpetual motion."

"Three of my friends have made perpetual motion machines," began our unwanted visitor rather stuffily. Harry didn't let him get any further: he just steamed on and ignored the interruption.

"Now our Australian Dr. Cavor wasn't searching for antigravity, or anything like it. In pure science, you can be pretty sure that nothing fundamental is ever discovered by anyone who's actually looking for it—that's half the fun of the game. Dr. Cavor was interested in producing atomic power: what he found was antigravity. And it was quite some time before he realised that was what he'd discovered.

"What happened, I gather, was this: The reactor was of a novel and rather daring design, and there was quite a possibility that it might blow up when the last pieces of fissile material were inserted. So it was assembled by remote control in one of Australia's numerous convenient deserts, all the final operations being observed through TV sets.

"Well, there was no explosion—which would have caused a nasty radio-active mess and wasted a lot of money, but wouldn't have damaged anything except a lot of reputations. What actually happened was much more unexpected, and much more difficult to explain.

"When the last piece of enriched uranium was inserted, the control rods pulled out, and the reactor brought up to criticality—everything went dead. The meters in the remote control room, two miles from the reactor, all dropped back to zero. The TV screen went blank. Cavor and his colleagues waited for the bang, but there wasn't one. They looked at each other for a moment with many wild surmises: then, without a word, they climbed up out of the buried control chamber.

"The reactor building was completely unchanged: it sat out there in the desert, a commonplace cube of brick holding a million pounds worth of fissile material and several years of careful design and development. Cavor wasted no time: he grabbed the jeep, switched on a portable Geiger counter, and hurried off to see what had happened.

"He recovered consciousness in hospital a couple of hours later. There was little wrong with him apart from a bad headache, which was nothing to the one his experiment was going to give him during the next few days. It seemed that when he got to within twenty feet of the reactor, his jeep had hit something with a terrific crash. Cavor had got tangled in the steering wheel and had a nice collection of bruises: the Geiger counter, oddly enough, was quite undamaged and was still clucking away quietly to itself, detecting no more than the normal cosmic-ray background.

"Seen from a distance, it had looked a perfectly normal sort of accident, that might have been caused by the jeep going into a rut. But Cavor hadn't been driving all that fast, luckily for him, and anyway there was no rut at the scene of the crash. What the jeep had run into was something quite impossible. It was an invisible wall, apparently the lower rim of a hemispherical dome, which entirely surrounded the reactor. Stones thrown up in the air slid back to the ground along the surface of this dome, and it also extended underground as far as digging could be carried out. It seemed as if the reactor was at the exact center of an impenetrable, spherical shell.

"Of course, this was marvellous news and Cavor was out of bed in no time, scattering nurses in all directions. He had no idea what had happened, but it was a lot more exciting than the humdrum piece of nuclear engineering that had started the whole business.

"By now you're probably all wondering what the devil a sphere of force—as you science-fiction writers would call it—has to do with antigravity. So I'll jump several days and give you the answers that Cavor and his team discovered only after much hard work and the consumption of many gallons of that potent Australian beer.

"The reactor, when it had been energised, had somehow produced an antigravity field. All the matter inside a twenty-foot-radius sphere had been made weightless, and the enormous amount of energy needed to do this had been extracted, in some utterly mysterious manner, from the uranium in the pile. Calculations showed that the amount of energy in the reactor was just sufficient to do the job. Presumably the sphere of force would have been larger still if there had been more ergs available in the power-source.

"I can hear someone just waiting to ask a question, so I'll anticipate them. Why didn't this weightless sphere of earth and air float up into space? Well, the earth was held together by its cohesion, anyway, so there was no reason why it should go wandering off. As for the air, that was forced to stay inside the zone of zero-gravity for a most surprising and subtle reason which leads me to the crux of this whole peculiar business.

"Better fasten your seat-belts for the next bit: we've got a bumpy passage ahead. Those of you who know something about potential theory won't have any trouble, and I'll do my best to make it as easy as I can for the rest.

"People who talk glibly about antigravity seldom stop to consider its implications, so let's look at a few fundamentals. As I've already said, weight implies energy—lots of it. That energy is entirely due to Earth's gravity field. *If you remove an object's weight*, that's precisely equivalent to taking it clear outside Earth's gravity. And any rocket engineer will tell you how much energy *that* requires."

Harry turned to me and said: "There's an analogy I'd like to borrow from one of your books, Arthur, that puts across the point I'm trying to make. You know—comparing the fight against Earth's gravity to climbing out of a deep pit."

"You're welcome," I said. "I pinched it from Doc Richardson, anyway."

"Oh," replied Harry. "I thought it was too good to be original. Well, here we go. If you hang on to this really very simple idea, you'll be O.K. To take an object clear away from the Earth requires as much work as lifting it *four thousand miles* against the steady drag of normal gravity. Now the matter inside Cavor's zone of force was still on the Earth's surface, but it was weightless. From the energy point of view, therefore, it was outside the Earth's gravity field. It was inaccessible as if it was on top of a four thousand mile high mountain.

"Cavor could stand outside the anti-gravity zone and look into it from a point a few inches away. To cross those few inches, he would have to do as much work as if he climbed Everest seven hundred times. It wasn't surprising that the jeep stopped in a hurry. No material object had stopped it, but from the point of view of dynamics it had run smack into a cliff four thousand miles high . . .

"I can see some blank looks that are not entirely due to the lateness of the hour. Never mind: if you don't get all this, just take my word for it. It won't spoil your appreciation of what follows—at least, I hope not.

"Cavor had realised at once that he had made one of the most important discoveries of the age, though it was some time before he worked out just what was going on. The final clue to the anti-gravitational nature of the field came when they shot a rifle bullet into it and observed the trajectory with a high-speed camera. Ingenious, don't you think?

"The next problem was to experiment with the field's generator and to find just what had happened inside the reactor when it had been switched on. This was a problem indeed. The reactor was there in plain sight, twenty feet away. But to reach it would require slightly more energy than going to the Moon. . . .

"Cavor was not disheartened by this, nor by the inexplicable failure of the reactor to respond to any of its remote controls. He theorised that it had been completely drained of energy, if one can use a rather misleading term, and that little if any power was needed to maintain the antigravity field once it had been set up. This was one of the many things that could only be determined by examination on the spot. So by hook or by crook, Dr. Cavor would have to go there.

"His first idea was to use an electrically-driven trolley, supplied with power through cables which it dragged behind it as it advanced into the field. A hundred horse-power generator, running continuously for seventeen hours, would supply enough energy to take a man of average weight on the perilous twenty-foot journey. A velocity of slightly over a foot an hour did not seem much to boast about, until you remembered that advancing one foot into the antigravity field was equivalent to a two hundred mile vertical climb.

"The theory was sound, but in practice the electric trolley wouldn't work. It started to push its way into the field, but began to skid after it had traversed half an inch. The reason was obvious when one started to think about it. Though the power was there, the traction wasn't. No wheeled vehicle could climb a gradient of two hundred miles per foot.

"This minor setback did not discourage Dr. Cavor. The answer, he realised at once, was to produce the traction at a point outside the field. When you wanted to lift a load vertically, you didn't use a cart: you used a jack or an hydraulic ram.

"The result of this argument was one of the oddest vehicles ever built. A small but comfortable cage, containing sufficient provisions to last a man for several days, was mounted at the end of a twenty-foot-long horizontal girder. The whole device was supported off the ground by balloon tires, and the theory was that the cage could be pushed right into the center of the field by a machine which would remain outside its influence. After some thought, it was decided that the best prime-mover would be the common or garden bulldozer.

"A test was made with some rabbits in the passenger compartment—and I can't help thinking that there was an interesting psychological point here. The experimenters were trying to get it both ways: as scientists they'd be pleased if their subjects got back alive, and as Australians they'd be just as happy if they got back dead. But perhaps I'm being a little too fanciful . . . (You know, of course, how Australians feel about rabbits.)

"The bulldozer chugged away hour after hour, forcing the weight of the girder and its insignificant payload up the enormous gradient. It was an uncanny sight—all this energy being expended to move a couple of rabbits twenty feet across a perfectly horizontal plain. The subjects of the experiment could be observed throughout the operation: they seemed to be perfectly happy and quite unaware of their historic rôle.

"The passenger compartment reached the centre of the field, was held there for an hour, and then the girder was slowly backed out again. The rabbits were alive, in good health, and to nobody's particular surprise there were now six of them.

"Dr. Cavor, naturally, insisted on being the first human being to venture into a zero-gravity field. He loaded up the compartment with torsion balances, radiation detectors, and periscopes so that he could look into the reactor when he finally got to it. Then he gave the signal, the bulldozer started chugging, and the strange journey began.

"There was, naturally, telephone communications from the passenger compartment to the outside world. Ordinary sound waves couldn't cross the barrier, for reasons which were still a little obscure, but radio and telephone both worked without difficulty. Cavor kept up a running commentary as he was edged forward into the field, describing his own reactions and relaying instrument readings to his colleagues.

"The first thing that happened to him, though he had expected it, was nevertheless rather unsettling. During the first few inches of his advance, as he moved through the fringe of the field, the direction of the vertical seemed to swing around. 'Up' was no longer toward the sky: it was now in the direction of the reactor hut. To Cavor, it felt as if he was being pushed up the face of a vertical cliff, with the reactor twenty feet above him. For the first time, his eyes and his ordinary human senses told him the same story as his scientific training. He could *see* that the centre of the field was, gravity-wise, higher than the place from which he had come. However, imagination still boggled at the thought of all the energy it would need to climb that innocent-looking twenty feet, and the hundreds of gallons of diesel fuel that must be burned to get him there.

"There was nothing else of interest to report on the journey itself, and at last, twenty hours after he had started, Cavor arrived at his destination. The wall of the reactor hut was right beside him, though to him it seemed not a wall but an unsupported floor sticking out at right angles from the cliff up which he had risen. The entrance was just above his head, like a trapdoor through which he would have to climb. This would present no great difficulty, for Dr. Cavor was an energetic young man, extremely eager to find just how he had created this miracle.

"Slightly too eager, in fact. For as he tried to work his way into the door, he slipped and fell off the platform that had carried him there.

"That was the last anyone ever saw of him—but it wasn't the last they heard of him. Oh dear no! He made a very big noise indeed . . .

"You'll see why when you consider the situation in which this unfortunate scientist now found himself. Hundreds of kilowatt-hours of energy had been pushed into him—enough to lift him to the Moon and beyond. All that work had been needed to take him to a point of zero gravitational potential. As soon as he lost his means of support, that energy began to reappear. To get back to our earlier and very picturesque analogy—the poor doctor had slipped off the edge of the four-thousand-mile-high mountain he had ascended.

"He fell back the twenty feet that had taken almost a day to climb. 'Ah, what a fall was there, my countrymen!' It was precisely equivalent, in terms of energy, to a free drop from the remotest stars down to the surface of the Earth. And you all know how much velocity an object acquires in *that* fall. It's the same velocity that's needed to get it there in the first place—the famous velocity of escape. Seven miles a second, or twenty-five thousand miles an hour.

"That's what Dr. Cavor was doing by the time he got back to

his starting point. Or to be more accurate, that's the speed he involuntarily tried to reach. As soon as he passed Mach 1 or 2, however, air-resistance began to have its little say. Dr. Cavor's funeral pyre was the finest, and indeed, the only, meteor display ever to take place entirely at sea level. . . .

"I'm sorry that this story hasn't got a happy ending. In fact, it hasn't got an ending at all, because that sphere of zero gravitational potential is still sitting there in the Australian desert, apparently doing nothing at all but in fact producing ever-increasing amounts of frustration in scientific and official circles. I don't see *how* the authorities can hope to keep it secret much longer. Sometimes I think how odd it is that the world's tallest mountain is in Australia—and that though it's four thousand miles high the airliners often fly right over it without knowing it's there."

You will hardly be surprised to hear that H. Purvis finished his narration at this point: even he could hardly take it much further, and no-one wanted him to. We were all, including his most tenacious critics, lost in admiring awe. I have since detected six fallacies of a fundamental nature in his description of Dr. Cavor's Frankensteinian fate, but at the time they never even occurred to me. (And I don't propose to reveal them now. They will be left, as the mathematics text-books put it, as an exercise for the reader.) What had earned our undying gratitude, however, was the fact that at some slight sacrifice of truth he had managed to keep Flying Saucers from invading the White Hart. It was almost closing time, and too late for our visitor to make a counter attack.

That is why the sequel seems a little unfair. A month later, someone brought a very odd publication to one of our meetings. It was nicely printed and laid out with professional skill, the misuse of which was sad to behold. The thing was called FLYING SAUCER REVELATIONS—and there on the front page was a full and detailed account of the story Purvis had told us. It was printed absolutely straight—and what was much worse than that, from poor Harry's point of view, was that it was attributed to him by name.

Since then he has had 4,375 letters on the subject, most of them from California. Twenty-four called him a liar; 4,205 believed him absolutely. (The remaining ones he couldn't decipher and their contents still remain a matter of speculation.)

I'm afraid he's never quite got over it, and I sometimes think he's going to spend the rest of his life trying to stop people believing the one story he never expected to be taken seriously.

There may be a moral here. For the life of me I can't find it.

Sleeping Beauty

It was one of those half-hearted discussions that is liable to get going in the "White Hart" when no-one can think of anything better to argue about. We were trying to recall the most extraordinary names we'd ever encountered, and I had just contributed "Obediah Polkinghorn" when—inevitably—Harry Purvis got into the act.

"It's easy enough to dig up odd names," he said, reprimanding us for our levity, "but have you ever stopped to consider a much more fundamental point—the *effects* of those names on their owners? Sometimes, you know, such a thing can warp a man's entire life. That is what happened to young Sigmund Snoring."

"Oh, no!" groaned Charles Willis, one of Harry's most implacable critics. "I don't believe it!"

"Do you imagine," said Harry indignantly, "that I'd *invent* a name like that? As a matter of fact, Sigmund's family name was something Jewish from Central Europe; it began with SCH and went on for quite a while in that vein. 'Snoring' was just an anglicised précis of it. However, all this is by the way; I wish people wouldn't make me waste time on such details."

Charlie, who is the most promising author I know (he has been promising for more than twenty-five years) started to make vaguely protesting noises, but someone public-spiritedly diverted him with a glass of beer.

"Sigmund," continued Harry, "bore his burden bravely enough until he reached manhood. There is little doubt, however, that his name preyed upon his mind, and finally produced what you might call a psycho-somatic result. If Sigmund had been born of any other parents, I am sure that he would not have become a sterterous and incessant snorer in fact as well as—almost—in name.

"Well, there are worse tragedies in life. Sigmund's family had a fair amount of money, and a sound-proofed bedroom protected the remainder of the household from sleepless nights. As is usually the case, Sigmund was quite unaware of his own nocturnal symphonies, and could never really understand what all the fuss was about.

"It was not until he got married that he was compelled to take his affliction—if you can call it that, for it only inflicted itself on other people—as seriously as it deserved. There is nothing unusual in a young bride returning from her honeymoon in a somewhat distracted condition, but poor Rachel Snoring had been through a uniquely shattering experience. She was red-eyed with lack of sleep, and any attempt to get sympathy from her friends only made them dissolve into peals of laughter. So it was not surprising that she gave Sigmund an ultimatum; unless he did something about his snoring, the marriage was off.

"Now this was a very serious matter both for Sigmund and his family. They were fairly well-to-do, but by no means rich—unlike Grand-uncle Reuben, who had died last year leaving a rather complicated will. He had taken quite a fancy to Sigmund, and had left a considerable sum of money in trust for him, which he would receive when he was thirty.

Unfortunately, Grand-uncle Reuben was very old-fashioned and strait-laced, and did not altogether trust the modern generation. One of the conditions of the bequest was that Sigmund should not be divorced or separated before the designated date. If he was, the money would go to found an orphanage in Tel Aviv.

"It was a difficult situation, and there is no way of guessing how it would have resolved itself had not someone suggested that Sigmund ought to go and see Uncle Hymie. Sigmund was not at all keen on this, but desperate predicaments demanded desperate remedies; so he went.

"Uncle Hymie, I should explain, was a very distinguished professor of physiology, and a Fellow of the Royal Society with a whole string of papers to his credit. He was also, at the moment, somewhat short of money, owing to a quarrel with the trustees of his college, and had been compelled to stop work on some of his pet research projects. To add to his annoyance, the Physics Department had just been given half a million pounds for a new synchrotron, so he was in no pleasant mood when his unhappy nephew called upon him.

"Trying to ignore the all-pervading smell of disinfectant and livestock, Sigmund followed the lab steward along rows of incomprehensible equipment, and past cages of mice and guinea-pigs, frequently averting his eyes from the revolting coloured diagrams which occupied so much wall-space. He found his uncle sitting at a bench, drinking tea from a beaker and absent-mindedly nibbling sandwiches.

" 'Help yourself,' he said ungraciously. 'Roast hamster—delicious. One of the litter we used for some cancer tests. What's the trouble?'

"Pleading lack of appetite, Sigmund told his distinguished uncle his tale of woe. The professor listened without much sympathy.

" 'Don't know what you got married for,' he said at last.

'Complete waste of time.' Uncle Hymie was known to possess strong views on this subject, having had five children but no wives. 'Still, we might be able to do something. How much money have you got?'

" 'Why?' asked Sigmund, somewhat taken aback. The professor waved his arms around the lab.

" 'Costs a lot to run all this,' he said.

" 'But I thought the university—'

" 'Oh yes—but any special work will have to be under the counter, as it were. I can't use college funds for it.'

" 'Well, how much will you need to get started?'

"Uncle Hymie mentioned a sum which was rather smaller than Sigmund had feared, but his satisfaction did not last for long. The scientist, it soon transpired, was fully acquainted with Grand-uncle Reuben's will; Sigmund would have to draw up a contract promising him a share of the loot when, in five years' time, the money became his. The present payment was merely an advance.

" 'Even so, I don't promise anything, but I'll see what can be done,' said Uncle Hymie, examining the cheque carefully. 'Come and see me in a month.'

"That was all that Sigmund could get out of him, for the professor was then distracted by a highly decorative research student in a sweater which appeared to have been sprayed on her. They started discussing the domestic affairs of the lab's rats in such terms that Sigmund, who was easily embarrassed, had to beat a hasty retreat.

"Now, I don't really think that Uncle Hymie would have taken Sigmund's money unless he was fairly sure he could deliver the goods. He must, therefore, have been quite near the completion of his work when the university had slashed his funds; certainly he could never have produced, in a mere four weeks, whatever complex mixture of chemicals it was that he injected into his hopeful nephew's arm a month after receiving the cash. The experiment was carried out at the professor's own home, late one evening; Sigmund was not too surprised to find the lady research student in attendance.

" 'What will this stuff *do*?' he asked.

" 'It will stop you snoring—I hope,' answered Uncle Hymie. 'Now, here's a nice comfortable seat, and a pile of magazines to read. Irma and I will take turns keeping an eye on you in case there are any side-reactions.'

" 'Side-reactions?' said Sigmund anxiously, rubbing his arm.

" 'Don't worry—just take it easy. In a couple of hours we'll know if it works.'

"So Sigmund waited for sleep to come, while the two scientists fussed around him (not to mention around each other) taking readings of blood-pressure, pulse, temperature and generally making Sigmund feel like a chronic invalid. When midnight arrived, he was not at all sleepy, but the professor and his assistant were almost dead on their feet. Sigmund realised that they had been working long hours on his behalf, and felt a gratitude which was quite touching during the short period while it lasted.

"Midnight came and passed. Irma folded up and the professor laid her, none too gently, on the couch. 'You're quite sure you don't feel tired yet?' he yawned at Sigmund.

" 'Not a bit. It's very odd; I'm usually fast asleep by this time.'

" 'You feel perfectly all right?'

" 'Never felt better.'

"There was another vast yawn from the professor. He muttered something like, 'Should have taken some of it myself,' then subsided into an armchair.

" 'Give us a shout," he said sleepily, 'if you feel anything unusual. No point in us staying up any longer.' A moment later Sigmund, still somewhat mystified, was the only conscious person in the room.

"He read a dozen copies of *Punch*, stamped 'Not to be Removed from the Common Room' until it was 2 a.m. He polished off all the *Saturday Evening Posts* by 4. A small bundle of *New Yorkers* kept him busy until 5, when he had a stroke of luck. An exclusive diet of caviar soon grows monotonous, and Sigmund was delighted to discover a limp and much-thumbed volume entitled 'The Blonde Was Willing'. This engaged his full attention until dawn, when Uncle Hymie gave a convulsive start, shot out of his chair, woke Irma with a well-directed slap, and then turned his full attention towards Sigmund.

" 'Well, my boy,' he said, with a hearty cheerfulness that at once alerted Sigmund's suspicions, 'I've done what you wanted. You passed the night without snoring, didn't you?'

"Sigmund put down the Willing Blonde, who was now in a situation where her co-operation or lack of it would make no difference at all.

" 'I didn't snore,' he admitted. 'But I didn't sleep either.'

" 'You still feel perfectly wide awake?'

" 'Yes—I don't understand it at all.'

"Uncle Hymie and Irma exchanged triumphant glances. 'You've made history, Sigmund,' said the professor. 'You're the first man to be able to do without sleep.' And so the news was broken to the astonished and not yet indignant guinea-pig.

"I know," continued Harry Purvis, not altogether accurately, "that many of you would like the scientific details of Uncle Hymie's discovery. But I don't know them, and if I did they would be too technical to give here. I'll merely point out, since I see some expressions which a less trusting man might describe as sceptical, that there is nothing really startling about such a development. Sleep, after all, is a highly variable factor. Look at Edison, who managed on two or three hours a day right up to the end of his life. It's true that men can't go without sleep indefinitely—but some animals can, so it clearly isn't a fundamental part of metabolism."

"*What* animals can go without sleep?" asked somebody, not so much in disbelief as out of pure curiosity.

"Well—er—of course!—the fish that live out in deep water beyond the continental shelf. If they ever fell asleep, they'd be snapped up by other fish, or they'd lose their trim and sink to the bottom. So they've got to keep awake all of their lives."

(I am still, by the way, trying to find if this statement of Harry's is true. I've ever caught him out yet on a scientific fact, though once or twice I've had to give him the benefit of the doubt. But back to Uncle Hymie.)

"It took some time," continued Harry, "for Sigmund to realise what an astonishing thing had been done to him. An enthusiastic commentary from his uncle, enlarging upon all the glorious possibilities that had been opened up for him now that he had been freed from the tyranny of sleep, made it difficult to concentrate on the problem. But presently he was able to raise the question that had been worrying him. 'How long will this last?' he enquired.

"The professor and Irma looked at each other. Then Uncle Hymie coughed a little nervously and replied: 'We're not quite sure yet. That's one thing we've got to find out. It's perfectly possible that the effect will be permanent.'

" 'You mean that I'll never be able to sleep again?'

" 'Not "Never be able to." "Never *want* to." However, I could probably work out some way of reversing the process if you're really anxious. Cost a lot of money, though.'

"Sigmund left hastily, promising to keep in touch and to report his progress every day. His brain was still in a turmoil, but first he had to find his wife and to convince her that he would never snore again.

"She was quite willing to believe him, and they had a touching reunion. But in the small hours of next morning it got very dull lying there with no-one to talk to, and presently Sigmund tiptoed away from his sleeping wife. For the first time, the full reality of his position was beginning to dawn upon him; what on earth was he going to do with the extra eight hours a day that had descended upon him as an unwanted gift?

"You might think that Sigmund had a wonderful—indeed an unprecedented—opportunity for leading a fuller life by acquiring that culture and knowledge which we all feel we'd like—if only we had the time to do something about it. He could read every one of the great classics that are just names to most people; he could study art, music or philosophy, and fill his mind with all the finest treasures of the human intellect. In fact, a good many of you are probably envying him right now.

"Well, it didn't work out that way. The fact of the matter is that even the highest grade mind needs some relaxation, and cannot devote itself to serious pursuits indefinitely. It was true that Sigmund had no further need of sleep, but he needed entertainment to occupy him during the long, empty hours of darkness.

"Civilisation, he soon discovered, was not designed to fit the requirements of a man who couldn't sleep. He might have been better off in Paris or New York, but in London practically everything closed down at 11 p.m., only a few coffee-bars were still open at midnight, and by 1 a.m.—well, the less said about any establishments still operating, the better.

"At first, when the weather was good, he occupied his time going for long walks, but after several encounters with inquisitive and sceptical policemen he gave this up. So he took to the car and drove all over London during the small hours, discovering all sorts of odd places he never knew existed. He soon had a nodding acquaintance with many night-watchmen, Covent Garden porters, and milkmen, as well as Fleet Street journalists and printers who had to work while the rest of the world slept. But as Sigmund was not the sort of person who took a great interest in his fellow human beings, this amusement soon palled and he was thrown back upon his own limited resources.

"His wife, as might be expected, was not at all happy about his nocturnal wanderings. He had told her the whole story, and though she had found it hard to believe she was forced to accept the evidence of her own eyes. But having done so, it seemed that she would prefer a husband who snored and stayed at home to one who tip-toed away around midnight and was not always back by breakfast.

"This upset Sigmund greatly. He had spent or promised a good deal of money (as he kept reminding Rachel) and taken a considerable personal risk to cure himself of his malaise. And was she grateful? No; she just wanted an itemised account of the time he spent when he should have been sleeping but wasn't. It was most unfair and showed a lack of trust which he found very disheartening.

"Slowly the secret spread through a wider circle, though the Snorings (who were a very close-knit clan) managed to keep it inside the family. Uncle Lorenz, who was in the diamond business, suggested that Sigmund take up a second job as it seemed a pity to waste all that additional working time. He produced a list of one-man occupations, which could be carried on equally easily by day or night, but Sigmund thanked him kindly and said he saw no reason why he should pay two lots of income tax.

"By the end of six weeks of twenty-four-hour days, Sigmund had had enough. He felt he couldn't read another book, go to another nightclub or listen to another gramophone record. His great gift, which many foolish men would have paid a fortune to possess, had become an intolerable burden. There was nothing to do but to go and see Uncle Hymie again.

"The professor had been expecting him, and there was no need to threaten legal proceedings, to appeal to the solidarity of the Snorings, or to make pointed remarks about breach of contract.

" 'All right, all right,' grumbled the scientist. 'I don't believe in casting pearls before swine. I knew you'd want the antidote sooner or later, and because I'm a generous man it'll only cost you fifty guineas. But don't blame me if you snore worse than ever.'

" 'I'll take that risk,' said Sigmund. As far as he and Rachel were concerned, it had come to separate rooms anyway by this time.

"He averted his gaze as the professor's assistant (not Irma this time, but an angular brunette) filled a terrifyingly large hypodermic with Uncle Hymie's latest brew. Before he had absorbed half of it, he had fallen asleep.

"For once, Uncle Hymie looked quite disconcerted. 'I didn't expect it to act *that* fast,' he said. 'Well, let's get him to bed—we can't have him lying around the lab.'

"By next morning, Sigmund was still fast asleep and showed no reactions to any stimuli. His breathing was imperceptible; he seemed to be in a trance rather than a slumber, and the professor was getting a little alarmed.

"His worry did not last for long, however. A few hours later an angry guinea-pig bit him on the finger, blood-poisoning set in, and the editor of *Nature* was just able to get the obituary notice into the current issue before it went to press.

"Sigmund slept through all this excitement and was still blissfully unconscious when the family got back from the Golders Green Crematorium and assembled for a council of war. *De mortuis nil nisi bonum*, but it was obvious that the late Professor Hymie had made another unfortunate mistake, and no-one knew how to set about unravelling it.

"Cousin Meyer, who ran a furniture store in the Mile End Road, offered to take charge of Sigmund if he could use him on display in his shop window to demonstrate the luxury of the beds he stocked. However, it was felt that this would be too undignified, and the family vetoed the scheme.

"But it gave them ideas. By now they were getting a little fed up with Sigmund; this flying from one extreme to another was really too much. So why not take the easy way out and, as one wit expressed it, let sleeping Sigmunds lie?

"There was no point in calling in another expensive expert who might only make matters worse (though how, no-one could quite imagine). It cost nothing to feed Sigmund, he required only a modicum of medical attention, and while he was sleeping there was certainly no danger of him breaking the terms of Grand-uncle Reuben's will. When this argument was rather tactfully put to Rachel, she quite saw the strength of it. The policy demanded required a certain amount of patience, but the ultimate reward would be considerable.

"The more Rachel examined it, the more she liked the idea. The thought of being a wealthy near-widow appealed to her; it had such interesting and novel possibilities. And, to tell the truth, she had had quite enough of Sigmund to last her for the five years until he came into his inheritance.

"In due course that time arrived and Sigmund became a semi-demi-millionaire. However, he still slept soundly—and in all those five years he had never snored once. He looked so peaceful lying there that it seemed a pity to wake him up, even if anyone knew exactly how to set about it. Rachel felt strongly that ill-advised tampering might have unfortunate consequences, and the family, after assuring itself that she could only get at the interest on Sigmund's fortune and not at the capital, was inclined to agree with her.

"And that was several years ago. When I last heard of him, Sigmund was still peacefully sleeping, while Rachel was having a perfectly wonderful time on the Riviera. She is quite a shrewd woman, as you may have guessed, and I think she realises how convenient it might be to have a youthful husband in cold storage for her old age.

"There are times, I must admit, when I think it's rather a pity that Uncle Hymie never had a chance of revealing his remarkable discoveries to the world. But Sigmund proved that our civilisation isn't yet ripe for such changes, and I hope I'm not around when some other physiologist starts the whole thing all over again."

Harry looked at the clock. "Good lord!" he exclaimed, "I'd no idea it was so late—I feel half asleep." He picked up his brief-case, stifled a yawn, and smiled benignly at us.

"Happy dreams, everybody," he said.

The Defenestration of Ermintrude Inch

And now I have a short, sad duty to perform. One of the many mysteries about Harry Purvis—who was so informative in every other direction—was the existence or otherwise of a Mrs. Purvis. It was true that he wore no wedding ring, but that means little nowadays. Almost as little, as any hotel proprietor will tell you, as does the reverse.

In a number of his tales, Harry had shown distinct evidence of some hostility towards what a Polish friend of mine, whose command of English did not match his gallantry, always referred to as ladies of the female sex. And it was by a curious coincidence that the very last story he ever told us first indicated, and then proved conclusively, Harry's marital status.

I do not know who brought up the word "defenestration", which is not, after all, one of the most commonly used abstract nouns in the language. It was probably one of the alarmingly erudite younger members of the "White Hart" clientele; some of them are just out of college, and so make us old-timers feel very callow and ignorant. But from the word, the discussion naturally passed to the deed. Had any of us ever been defenestrated? Did we know anyone who had?

"Yes," said Harry. "It happened to a verbose lady I once knew. She was called Ermintrude, and was married to Osbert Inch, a sound engineer at the B.B.C.

"Osbert spent all his working hours listening to other people talking, and most of his free time listening to Ermintrude. Unfortunately, he couldn't switch *her* off at the turn of a knob, and so he very seldom had a chance of getting a word in edgeways.

"There are some women who appear sincerely unaware of the fact that they cannot stop talking, and are most surprised when anyone accuses them of monopolising the conversation. Ermintrude would start as soon as she woke up, change gear so that she could hear herself speak above the eight o'clock news, and continue unabated until Osbert thankfully left for work. A couple of years of this had almost reduced him to a nervous wreck, but one morning when his wife was handicapped by a long overdue attack of laryngitis he made a spirited protest against her vocal monopoly.

"To his incredulous disbelief, she flatly refused to accept the charge. It appeared that to Ermintrude, time ceased to exist when *she* was talking—but she became extremely restive when anyone else held the stage. As soon as she had recovered her voice, she told Osbert how unfair it was of him to make such an unfounded accusation, and the argument would have been very acrimonious—if it had been possible to have an argument with Ermintrude at all.

"This made Osbert an angry and also a desperate man. But he was an ingenious one, too, and it occurred to him that he could produce irrefutable evidence that Ermintrude talked a hundred words for every syllable he was able to utter. I mentioned that he was a sound engineer, and his room was fitted up with Hi-Fi set, tape recorder, and the usual electronic tools of his trade, some of which the B.B.C. had unwittingly supplied.

"It did not take him very long to construct a piece of equipment which one might call a Selective Word Counter. If you know anything about audio engineering you'll appreciate how it could be done with suitable filters and dividing circuits—and if you don't, you'll have to take it for granted. What the apparatus did was simply this; a microphone picked up every word spoken in the Inch apartment, Osbert's deeper tones went one way and registered on a counter marked "His," and Ermintrude's higher frequencies went the other direction and ended up on the counter marked "Hers."

"Within an hour of switching on, the score was as follows:—

His	23
Hers	2,530

"As the numbers flickered across the counter dials, Ermintrude became more and more thoughtful and at the same time more and more silent. Osbert, on the other hand, drinking the heady wine of victory (though to anyone else it would have looked like his morning cup of tea) began to make the most of his advantage and became quite talkative. By the time he had left for work, the counters had reflected the changing status in the household:—

His	1,043
Hers	3,397

"Just to show who was now the boss, Osbert left the apparatus switched on; he had always wondered if Ermintrude talked to herself as a purely automatic reflex even when there was no-one around to hear what she was saying. He had, by the way, thoughtfully taken the precaution of putting a lock on the Counter so that his wife couldn't turn it off while he was out.

"He was a little disappointed to find that the figures were

quite unaltered when he came home that evening, but thereafter the score soon started to mount again. It became a kind of game—though a deadly serious one—with each of the protagonists keeping one eye on the machine whenever either of them said a word. Ermintrude was clearly discomfited; ever and again she would suffer a verbal relapse and increase her score by a couple of hundred before she brought herself to a halt by a supreme effort of self-control. Osbert, who still had such a lead that he could afford to be garrulous, amused himself by making occasional sardonic comments which were well worth the expenditure of a few-score points.

"Although a measure of equality had been restored in the Inch household, the Word Counter had, if anything, increased the state of dissension. Presently Ermintrude, who had a certain natural intelligence which some people might have called craftiness, made an appeal to her husband's better nature. She pointed out that neither of them was really behaving naturally while every word was being monitored and counted; Osbert had unfairly let her get ahead and was now being taciturn in a way that he would never have been had he not got that warning score continuously before his eyes. Though Osbert gagged at the sheer effrontery of this charge, he had to admit that the objection did contain an element of truth. The test would be fairer and more conclusive if neither of them could see the accumulating score—if, indeed, they forgot all about the presence of the machine and so behaved perfectly naturally, or at least as naturally as they could in the circumstances.

"After much argument they came to a compromise. Very sportingly, in his opinion, Osbert reset the dials to zero and sealed up the counter windows so that no-one could take a peek at the scores. They agreed to break the wax seals—on which they had both impressed their fingerprints—at the end of the week, and to abide by the decision. Concealing the microphone under a table, Osbert moved the counter equipment itself into his little workshop, so that the living-room now bore no sign of the implacable electronic watchdog that was controlling the destiny of the Inches.

"Thereafter, things slowly returned to normal. Ermintrude became as talkative as ever, but now Osbert didn't mind in the least because he knew that every word she uttered was being patiently noted to be used as evidence against her. At the end of the week, his triumph would be complete. He could afford to allow himself the luxury of a couple of hundred words a day, knowing that Ermintrude used up this allowance in five minutes.

"The breaking of the seals was performed ceremonially at the end of an unusually talkative day, when Ermintrude had repeated verbatim three telephone conversations of excruciating banality which, it seemed, had occupied most of her afternoon. Osbert had merely smiled and said "Yes, dear" at ten minute intervals, meanwhile trying to imagine what excuse his wife would put forward when confronted by the damning evidence.

"Imagine, therefore, his feelings when the seals were removed to disclose the week's total:

His	143,567
Hers	32,590

"Osbert stared at the incredible figures with stunned disbelief. *Something* had gone wrong—but where? There must, he decided, have been a fault in the apparatus. It was annoying, very annoying, for he knew perfectly well that Ermintrude would never let him live it down, even if he proved conclusively that the Counter had gone haywire.

"Ermintrude was still crowing victoriously when Osbert pushed her out of the room and started to dismantle his errant equipment. He was half-way through the job when he noticed something in his waste-paper basket which he was sure he hadn't put there. It was a closed loop of tape, a couple of feet long, and he was quite unable to account for its presence as he had not used the tape-recorder for several days. He picked it up, and as he did so suspicion exploded into certainty.

"He glanced at the recorder; the switches, he was quite sure, were not as he had left them. Ermintrude was crafty, but she was also careless. Osbert had often complained that she never did a job properly, and here was the final proof.

"His den was littered with old tapes carrying unerased test passages he had recorded; it had been no trouble at all for Ermintrude to locate one, snip off a few words, stick the ends together, switch to "Playback" and leave the machine running hour after hour in front of the microphone. Osbert was furious with himself for not having thought of so simple a ruse; if the tape had been strong enough, he would probably have strangled Ermintrude with it.

"Whether he tried to do anything of the sort is still uncertain. All we know is that she went out of the apartment window, and of course it could have been an accident—but there was no way of asking her, as the Inches lived four storeys up.

"I know that defenestration is usually deliberate, and the Coroner had some pointed words to say on the subject. But nobody could prove that Osbert pushed her, and the whole thing soon blew over. About a year later he married a charming little deaf-and-dumb girl, and they're one of the happiest couples I know."

There was a long pause when Harry had finished, whether out of disbelief or out of respect for the late Mrs. Inch it would be hard to say. But before anyone could make a suitable comment, the door was thrown open and a formidable blonde advanced into the private bar of the "White Hart".

It is seldom indeed that life arranges its climaxes as neatly as this. Harry Purvis turned very pale and tried, in vain, to hide himself in the crowd. He was instantly spotted and pinned down beneath a barrage of invective.

"So *this*," we heard with interest, "is where you've been giving your Wednesday evening lectures on quantum mechanics! I should have checked up with the University years ago! Harry Purvis, you're a liar, and I don't mind if everybody knows it. And as for your friends"—she gave us all a scathing look—"it's a long time since I've seen such a scruffy lot of tipplers."

"Hey, just a minute!" protested Drew from the other side of the counter. She quelled him with a glance, then turned upon poor Harry again.

"Come along," she said, "you're going home. No, you needn't finish that drink! I'm sure you've already had more than enough."

Obediently, Harry Purvis picked up his brief-case and coat.

"Very well, Ermintrude," he said meekly.

. . . .

I will not bore you with the long and still unsettled argument as to whether Mrs Purvis really was called Ermintrude, or whether Harry was so dazed that he automatically applied the name to her. We all have our theories about that, as indeed we have about everything concerning Harry. All that matters now is the sad and indisputable fact that no-one has ever seen him since that evening.

It is just possible that he doesn't know where we meet nowadays, for a few months later the "White Hart" was taken over by a new management and we all followed Drew lock, stock and barrel—particularly barrel—to his new establishment. Our weekly sessions now take place at the "Sphere," and for a long time many of us used to look up hopefully when the door opened to see if Harry had managed to escape and find his way back to us. It is, indeed, partly in the hope that he will see this book and hence discover our new location that I have gathered these tales together.

Even those who never believed a word you spoke miss you, Harry. If you have to defenestrate Ermintrude to regain your freedom, do it on a Wednesday evening between six and eleven, and there'll be forty people in the "Sphere" who'll provide you with an alibi. But get back *somehow*; things have never been quite the same since you went.

Charles Adams

ABOUT THE AUTHOR

ARTHUR C. CLARKE was born in Minehead, England, in 1917 and was made a Freeman of his hometown in 1992. He now lives in Sri Lanka, where he was the first person to be granted "Resident Guest" status. He is a graduate, and Fellow, of King's College, London, and Chancellor of the International Space University and the University of Moratuwa, near which the Government has established the Arthur C. Clarke Institute for Modern Technologies.

Sir Arthur has twice been Chairman of the British Interplanetary Society. While serving as an RAF radar officer in 1945, he published the theory of communications satellites, most of which operate in what is now called the Clarke Orbit. The impact of this invention upon global politics resulted in his nomination for the 1994 Nobel Peace Prize.

He has written over seventy books and shared an Oscar nomination with Stanley Kubrick for the movie based on his novel *2001: A Space Odyssey*.

His *Mysterious World*, *Strange Powers*, and *Mysterious Universe TV* series have been shown worldwide.

His many honors include the Marconi and Lindbergh Awards, as well as three Hugos and three Nebulas for his science fiction. In a global satellite ceremony in 1995, he received NASA's highest civilian honor, its Distinguished Public Service Medal.

Sir Arthur's recreations are scuba diving on Indian Ocean wrecks with his company, Underwater Safaris, table tennis (despite Post Polio Syndrome), observing the Moon through his fourteen-inch telescope, and playing with his Chihuahua, "Pepsi," and his six computers.

He received the Vidya Jyothi ("Light of Science") Award from the president of Sri Lanka in 1986, and the CBE (Commander of the British Empire) from H.M. Queen Elizabeth in 1989. And in 1996 he went to Beijing to receive the International Academy of Astronautics' highest honor, the von Karman Award.

Sir Arthur was made a knight in the Queen's 1998 New Year's Honours List for his "services to literature."